USED *Cookie* SHEETS

Used Cookie Sheets: Very Short Stories
Copyright ©2021 by Lori Lipsky
Bamzyl Books LLC
Bamzylbooks.com
ISBN: 978-1-7365325-0-8 (paperback)
ISBN: 978-1-7365325-1-5 (eBook)

The following titles were originally published elsewhere, in slightly different form:

The Bookstore copyright © 2017 by Lori Lipsky
Shopping for Next Year copyright © 2018 by Lori Lipsky
The Interrogation Inconsistency copyright © 2019 by Lori Lipsky

For information, address Bamzyl Books, 7145 Mile Road, Sun Prairie, WI 53590

Written and compiled by Lori Lipsky
Cover, typesetting, and eBook design by Michelle Rayburn, missionandmedia.com

2021 First Edition

For my parents,

Neil and DorEtta

with gratitude and affection

USED Cookie SHEETS

Very Short Stories

Lori Lipsky

BAMZYL BOOKS

Contents

Only One Rachmaninoff

Every morning the boy set his timer to practice piano for an hour before school. His teacher offered him praise each week during his lesson. She'd say, "Great job today," or "Well done," or even "You're making terrific progress, and I'm proud of you."

One day, he overheard his parents in the kitchen talking about him.

"Sure, he practices, but I'm not awestruck."

"I guess he'll never be Rachmaninoff."

The child had never heard of Rachmaninoff, but he got the message. Music lessons soon met their end, and the piano-loving child lost his opportunity to show the world who he might become.

Junior

Momma was an insomniac. Her trouble with sleeping started way back before Junior was a teenager, and it never stopped. Junior never was the compliant sort of child. Momma did her best with discipline and consistency, but Auntie Lou says children grow to make their own choices. Junior, God bless him, chose that darned motorcycle the year after he got his license and ran it smack dab into the big old oak tree near the bottom of Hillcrest Road.

That old tree landed him in the hospital just long enough for Momma and me to come and see him one last time. His face looked about as perfect as ever—Junior always was the good-looking twin—but the doctor said to us as nice as he could that Junior's insides were beyond saving.

When we got to that hospital room, Junior opened his brown eyes with those long, curly lashes. He told Momma he loved her and that he was sorry about the motorcycle. He was sorry about everything. Momma told Junior to hush and save his strength to tell the Lord those things, but Junior said he'd already done that.

That's when I saw a tear fall from Momma's eye, and that's something I'd seldom seen before. Momma put her finger on Junior's lips and told him she loved him. Always had and always would. No matter what. She told him everything would be just fine and why didn't he rest. And what do you know, I noticed a change on Junior's face. For the first time in a long while, Junior listened to Momma. I saw his face relax, his mouth smile, and then he rested.

Momma says Junior is resting his eternal rest. She says, just like the one thief on a cross next to Jesus, Junior felt sorry for his sins before he died. There's no doubt about it, Momma says. She could tell by his tone of voice. She could see it on his face. I saw his face too because I drove Momma to the hospital that day, and I think Momma has the right idea.

I was right in the room with Junior during all those Sunday School classes, and the teachers at the Church on the Corner don't mess around. They teach right from the Bible. Junior, God rest his soul, heard all those words growing up just like I did.

Momma made sure we never missed a Sunday. We memorized the Lord's Prayer, the Apostle's Creed, John chapter 3, and Romans 12. We memorized a whole mess of Bible verses. So many I could never count. Pastor always said no boy was a better memorizer than Junior and that someday it would pay off.

Momma says Junior just got lost during his teen years. She says he would have grown out of it if he hadn't had his accident. I'm inclined to agree. If there's one thing I've learned, it's that Momma is usually right.

After the funeral and the burial, I headed back to school. Momma went to bed. Auntie Lou came over to stay with us for a while. She told me I should give Momma some space and time to grieve. Momma stayed in her bed for a whole month, sleeping and crying and praying. Auntie Lou brought food to her. I went in every night and gave her a kiss and a hug.

Then one day, Momma got up. She opened the curtains in her bedroom to let the light shine in again. Auntie Lou went on back to her home, and Momma and I got on with our lives. Momma said she'd done grieved for a month, but now the good Lord had living for her to do. "The Lord gives, and the Lord takes. Blessed be the name of the Lord," Momma would say over and over.

After a while, she set the words to music and went about the kitchen singing it.

On her first day up and around, Momma said it was good for her to remember the kindness of the Lord. Every morning, she planned to write down five things she was thankful for. The idea came to her from a magazine article she'd read in the doctor's office. Momma left the notebook open on the kitchen counter. Sure enough, she was true to her word. Momma kept that plan for the rest of her life.

Five years after Junior passed on, I got married and moved up north. Momma gave her blessing. She loved my Henry and said she could see we were a good fit. "I'm sorry to see you move away, but a couple needs to go where the jobs are. It's a great blessing you both found work. Bills surely need to be paid, and I've learned the good Lord can lead folks to new places through work. There's no doubt about that."

Momma often said our jobs were a great blessing from the Lord, even if they took us away from her. Maybe she repeated that thought to comfort herself. I know I found an awful lot of comfort in those words on the days when homesickness set in.

We visited Momma every Christmas. With the price of travel, that's all we could afford. After some years went by, I saved enough for a ticket for Momma so she could come for a nice long visit. The thought of sitting in a plane scared Momma, but she was excited to visit us in our northern home. She said she'd pray a lot, fight the fear, and fly anyway.

On the day she was to come visit, Momma got dressed, called for a taxi to take her to the airport, then pulled a chair over to the front window to watch and wait for the driver.

Auntie Lou found Momma later, sitting in the chair by the window, her hand resting on her suitcase. Momma never got to see me in our home in the north, but I like to think maybe the good Lord has given her a glimpse of it from heaven.

As Momma would say, "The good Lord knows what's best, and he knows how to give it."

Auntie Lou said when she found her, Momma's face looked all calm and peaceful, and she had just the sort of smile Momma always said Junior had when he passed on.

I like to think that Momma and Junior are together in heaven now. They have heaps to do there, but they've got lots to smile about too as they wait for me and Henry and my family to arrive. The thought of Momma in her special place in heaven puts a smile on my face. I'm sorry as sorry can be that she never got to see our far-away home or our babies that we waited years and years for. But for now, as Momma would say, I have plenty of living to do, and I best get to it.

Bedtime

Bill and Patti get ready for bed at nine o'clock. Bill wants to stay up later to finish watching the game, but Patti feels exhausted and needs to go to bed. Patti insists she cannot sleep until everyone is in bed, the lights are out, and the house is quiet. So, Bill goes to bed with her, even though the ballgame is important. The couple raised three kids in the house, but now it's just the two of them in their empty nest.

Bill would like to run the furnace fan. It does a good job of moving the air around. If they don't run it during the summer months, he wakes up after a few hours, and he's so hot he can't get back to sleep.

Patti can't stand the sound of the fan. She needs quiet

to sleep, so after years of hearing about it, Bill knows better than to turn the noisy fan on.

Patti would like to run their quiet bedroom ceiling fan to keep cool, but Bill wakes up with a sore neck every time, so she only uses it a few days each year when Bill is out of town on business. As a compromise, before Bill crawls into bed, he turns the air conditioning down two degrees. On hot and humid evenings, that's their agreement. Patti can bear to have the furnace fan run a short while, but not all night.

In winter, Bill piles extra blankets on his side. He wears pajama pants and a long-sleeved shirt to bed. He says his circulation isn't great. Patti can only sleep if they set the temperature down, and besides, she likes to be careful about the heating bill.

Patti sometimes suffers hot flashes at night. She wears the same short, sleeveless nightie in winter as she does in summer. Once in a while, she sweats so bad she wakes Bill up, and he helps her change the bedding. He wonders how in the world she can sweat when he's freezing, but he doesn't say much about it.

Twice, he's hinted he could move into the room their daughter used to have, but Patti says she can't sleep without him. And she'd be lonely. She hates it whenever he has to leave town on business. Good thing it's only once or twice a year.

Tonight, he thinks about sleeping in their daughter's

room just for the night, but before he mentions the possibility, Patti speaks.

"Don't you dare mention sleeping in Hannah's room, Bill. You know I need you here. You belong with me till death do we part."

Bill nods in the affirmative and repeats the words, "till death do we part." He gives her a hug and tells her he hopes they have many more years together in the same bed. And he means it.

Fruit Not Included

The four sat in the corner by the window. A young waitress approached and dropped menus on the table. Cathy passed them out.

"Do you have a gluten-free menu?" she asked. "I read on your website you have gluten-free options."

"I'm not sure."

"Could you ask someone who might know? I'm very gluten sensitive."

The server returned after several minutes.

"We have gluten-free bread for an extra dollar."

Cathy asked if the chips that came with the sandwich were gluten free.

"I'm not sure."

"Could you ask when you go back? If they don't have gluten, I'll have the chips. Otherwise, can you leave them off the plate? I'm very sensitive."

The server came back to fill their water glasses after about ten minutes. Cathy couldn't help herself. She was hungry and wanted to know if she'd be eating chips for lunch.

The young woman said, "Yeah, sorry. The cook says they're fried here on site in the same oil as the breaded chicken, so they might be contaminated."

"Oh, shoot. Can you bring me a dish of fruit instead?"

"Sorry, no substitutions."

"No need to substitute. Just leave the chips off. I'll pay whatever it costs for a side of fruit," Cathy said.

"Let me check if that's allowed."

Five minutes later, the four women received their sandwiches.

The plates were small. All four sandwiches were covered with potato chips. No fruit was served.

The Bookstore

Shannon stepped into their indoor pool room and called to her boys to finish their laps and take a shower. A stickler for routine, Shannon rose at six thirty every morning. Today she had finished her laps and pool exercise routine, letting the boys sleep in while she got some laundry done.

The swim meet had filled their weekend. With school closed and after-school swim practice canceled, Shannon planned to enjoy a late Monday morning at the bookstore with the boys, followed by a peaceful afternoon at home. The boys' friends across the street were gone for the long weekend. That suited her fine.

Seth and Noah dressed and got ready to go in less than ten minutes.

"Let's head to the bookstore, guys. We can sit around, read for a couple of hours, and then head home for lunch and a movie." The plan was a regular family favorite on days off. They all adored books.

"Can we get a smoothie to drink at the bookstore café since it's a special day? Just this once, Mom?"

"Grab a bottle of water or something from the garage fridge, Seth. Pick a snack too. We don't need to spend money at the café. Let's get going."

They knew the routine. All three browsed for a book and then seated themselves at the counter that faced the parking lot. They sat without a word for almost two hours, enjoying their reading time.

"I'm getting hungry," said Noah. "Can we have lunch here?"

Shannon looked at her watch. "It is getting close to lunchtime. Let's not spend money here. I'll make sandwiches at home. We can eat in the theater room and watch on the big screen."

"I'm starving," said Noah.

"I still have 170 pages to go, Mom," Seth said. "Can we buy our books today? Just this once?"

"We'll stop at the library on the way home." Shannon recognized the signs of hunger in Noah's slumped shoulders and fading cooperation. "It will only take a few minutes. Write your title and author here on this paper. It's right on the way. We'll hustle."

Later that evening, the three lounged in the solarium. The boys played video games on their phones. Shannon used hers to check the news.

"Oh, no! I can't believe it!" The boys played on as if they wore earplugs. "You guys are going to be devastated when you come out of your video game stupor."

"What, Mom?" Seth asked.

"Never mind. We'll commiserate later tonight when you're listening with both ears."

The article announced the closing of their favorite bookstore. The one they visited that morning.

The ad under the store name read:

> *Closing permanently on the 15th*
> *After twenty-eight years in business*
> *We held on as long as we could*
> *We will miss you, dear readers*
> *Thank you to our loyal customers*

The Kiss

On Monday morning, Matthew left for work at six o'clock as usual. Judy needs more sleep than her husband, so she gets up around seven. That morning, Judy woke with a start when her phone alarm went off. Locating the phone under her covers, she forced the horrible sound to stop. She tried to get back to her dream, but it was too late.

Judy had just caught Matthew kissing his old girl-friend when the blasted alarm went off. She needed to know what happened next.

The week prior, she and Matthew ran into his ex-girlfriend at their neighborhood diner. He said it was the first time he'd seen her in twenty years. That diner is forever ruined for Judy now that she knows how pretty and friendly Matthew's ex is.

The woman sat enjoying lunch with her husband and their two teenaged girls when Matthew noticed her in the next booth and introduced Judy. She thought the four seemed to be a happy family.

Why had Matthew kissed her in Judy's dream? What an awful thing for her to witness. Judy wasn't sure she could forgive Matthew. Maybe after her coffee she'd consider it. He'd better have a good explanation. If he weren't at work right now, she'd let him have it.

A Lawn Care Pause

H is wife opened the door and waved both arms at Carl to get his attention. When he stopped the mower, she called out to him. "Can you run to the store and pick up some fresh green beans and sweet corn?"

"Can't it wait? I'm right in the middle of mowing."

"I need them now so I can do the snapping and husking and everything. If you can't go, I will, but I don't want to leave my roast."

Carl came into the house and rinsed off his hands and face. As he opened the door to leave, his wife followed behind him into the garage. "You can't go to the store looking like that."

"What's wrong with me?"

"Aren't you going to shave that stubble?"

"It's Tuesday. No-shave Tuesday. Don't worry, dear. No one will see me." He rubbed the stubble on his face.

When he looked down at himself, he saw his favorite blue shirt with the tiny holes near his belly, his mowing pants he'd worn every time he cut the grass for the last three years, and his scruffy brown shoes.

"What about that ridiculous cap?"

"You wouldn't want this beautiful head to get sun-burned, would you?" He removed his cap, rubbed his balding head, replaced it, and then winked at her. She rolled her eyes at him in return.

"If you want me to go now, I'll have to go like this. I want to finish the yard before dinner, and I'll get cleaned up once I'm done. I don't have time to change and shave and all that nonsense."

"Fine. Just don't you dare run into anyone we know," she said as she wagged her finger at him.

"I'll do my best to remain invisible, ignore the world, and 'accept the consequences, whatever they may be.'"

"I hear the Auden quote in there, smarty-pants," she said. He pecked her on the cheek, gave her one of his winning smiles, and climbed into his pickup truck.

18

Carl needed a break from his work more than he realized. The air conditioning at the store on such a warm day was a bonus. Cutting an acre of grass on a hot summer afternoon might be a young man's game, he thought.

He took his time wandering through the supermarket. The produce department was on the opposite side of the store from where he had parked. Carl even made an extra-long route to browse the meat coolers. Sirloin steaks were on sale. He picked up a package. He'd have to mention the sale to his wife. The steaks looked delicious. Maybe she'd want to stock up. His wife enjoyed taking advantage of sales.

Carl picked up a package of bacon. He peered through the plastic window on the back of the package. He'd learned that trick from his wife over thirty years ago. The meat didn't look too fatty. Bacon for breakfast sounded heavenly. Carl wasn't sure if they were out of it at home or not, so he put the package back where he found it. He'd have to check their refrigerator meat drawer when he got home. He could always return tomorrow.

Time to get what I came for, he thought, as he looked at his still-empty shopping cart. Get thee to produce, old man.

"Excuse me, sir." Carl looked up to see a well-dressed woman with her hands on a shopping cart filled with groceries. She looked at him with a kind smile. Carl looked down at his shoes and heard his wife's words in his ears. He noticed his foot tapping, so he stopped it. Then he remembered his manners and reached to take his hat off but thought better of it when he recalled he'd saved his shower until after he finished cutting the grass. His hair would be a sight. He tipped his cap but left it on his head.

When the woman extended her arm toward him, he wiped his hands on his pants. He almost returned her handshake but drew back at the last moment when he noticed cash in her hand. "Could you use twenty dollars? I apologize for watching you, but I couldn't help but notice as you browsed the meat section," she said.

Carl's hands went into his pockets. He felt his face turn red. Still looking at his feet, he answered, "No, thank you, ma'am. But thanks anyway." He forced himself to look at the woman's eyes. Carl returned her smile, tipping his well-worn cap at her a second time. He pushed his empty cart toward the produce area to pick up the green beans and corn his wife sent him to buy.

As soon as Carl got home, he said to his wife, "You were right as always, dear. My ears were lazy. Next time I'd better pay attention to your advice and change my clothes first."

He explained to her what had happened. They laughed together about the incident throughout the evening. More than once, his wife said, "Carl, it does my heart good to know there are still generous people out there."

Honoring Van Gogh

Inspired to mimic a patron of the arts who allegedly made the only purchase of a Van Gogh painting during the artist's lifetime, Allison set aside a portion of her monthly earnings. She dedicated her new account to invest in work by living artists.

In search of the first piece for her planned collection, she discovered Tulips in a Mason Jar. The small oil painting, her first purchase of an original, now hangs in her office. She's determined her first acquisition will not be the living artist's only sale.

A Stay with Joyce

A year after Joyce's husband passed away, her poodle left her too. Maggie had followed her from room to room throughout the day, enjoying lengthy, peaceful naps whenever Joyce left to run errands, attend one of her club meetings, or have lunch with a friend.

The old dog suffered from car sickness. Even on the best weather days, Maggie couldn't accompany Joyce when she hopped into her old Mercedes. The used car was a birthday gift from her husband not long before he died.

Joyce had debated long and hard about getting a new dog when Maggie passed. Joyce's son, who called on the twenty-fifth of each month without fail, urged her to re-place the dog at once.

"I'll feel much better if you have a dog to keep you company and warn you of strangers on the property. You should get another dog, Mother."

"Maggie couldn't hear for her last four years, and her sight wasn't the best either. She wasn't much of a watch-dog, but she loved my company and loved to snuggle. I miss that."

"I didn't realize the dog was so old," her son said. He hadn't been to visit in over five years, and when he phoned, the conversation centered on him and his family. "Wow, he got old pretty fast."

"She was a fourteen-year-old female. It's been a while since you've visited," Joyce said. "I don't think another dog is in my future. That's behind me now. I'll miss her company, but I hated taking her to the vet and the groom-er. Whenever we drove up to either building, her anxiety got my anxiety going, and the two of us were a hot mess. I won't miss those times one bit."

Bev from church recommended dog fostering to Joyce. According to Bev, fostering was all the rage. Joyce nodded at the advice but inwardly tossed the suggestion aside. Her friend Cindy had fostered, but the experience turned from a good deed into a deed gone wrong.

Cindy and the dog weren't a compatible match. Neither liked the other, but when she tried to return the dog, the woman in charge guilted her into keeping it. Cindy was in her fourth year of sharing a home with a dog she didn't get along with, although the last time Joyce talked with Cindy, things had improved a bit. There was hope, but who wanted to spend four years of their life taking care of an ungrateful dog? Joyce didn't.

One of her book club friends suggested she try dog sitting. "You gain all the advantages of canine companionship with none of the vet and groomer hassles. The owner buys the food, cleans the teeth, trims the nails, and bathes the dog. The owner handles visits to the animal hospital, vaccinations, and everything else. To be safe, make sure you require owners to provide proof of vaccines. Boarding places do that, I think. And maybe you should insist the owners bathe the dog within one week of their stay if you want to invite the pup onto your bed. And I have a hunch you will."

Joyce took her friend's advice to heart and decided it might be a terrific idea. She'd try it and see how things went. The job would provide company, security, and walking companions. And she could say goodbye to vet visits and the other anxiety-producing aspects of pet ownership.

Best of all, she wouldn't have another canine best friend dying on her. That was the worst thing about dogs.

The very worst thing. They rarely outlived you. She didn't think she could bear the pain of losing another best friend.

It was ridiculous, she knew, but Joyce hadn't even considered the financial repercussions of opening a dog-sitting business before she began the process. Now that she was two years into it, she'd learned a pleasant lesson— the money was a huge, unexpected benefit. Living in a neighborhood with so many young families proved to be the perfect situation. She required no marketing budget. All of her business came by word of mouth. Joyce had never been shy, and in this case, talking paid. Her business took off.

Every home around had a dog, it seemed, and since she'd researched and priced herself below market, she found she had plenty of business. Right now, her calendar was booked eight weeks out.

After all, what family wouldn't want to have their dog stay with Joyce? She didn't host more than two pets at a time. She took them on at least one long walk every day, and dogs could sleep in their own crate from home, on Joyce's sofa, or in her king-sized bed with her. From a dog's point of view, a stay with Joyce was pure luxury. It beat the nearest boarding facility—crates stacked on top of one another, with dogs voicing their unhappiness throughout the day.

Joyce sent a minimum of two photos per day to the vacationing families, including cheery updates on their dog's condition.

Rover enjoyed a late morning nap on the screened-in patio.

Rover seems to love being scratched behind the ears.

Rover enjoyed catching the ball this morning in my fenced-in backyard.

Rover plopped down and snuggled with me during my four o'clock television break.

Besides the money, Joyce was reaping the benefits of getting to know those who lived nearby. Neighbors called to set up appointments and stayed on the line to chat once in a while. Most in the neighborhood knew her by name now because she was outside dog-walking so often.

The extrovert in her enjoyed the opportunity to stop and visit with neighbors as she passed their homes. Maggie hadn't been energetic enough to take walks in her last few years, so Joyce's social life leaped forward now with all her strolls around the neighborhood.

She was excited to have resigned from retirement. After working in a bank for thirty years, this job was a delightful change. It didn't even seem like work to her. She saved most of her earnings in a designated savings account, minus her usual tithe.

Joyce had dreamed of owning a Mercedes all her adult life, and her husband made sure that dream of hers came true the year before he passed away. But the car had been ten years old, with ninety thousand miles on the odometer when he'd purchased it. And that was four years ago. She knew her old car couldn't last forever.

The money from her business venture would allow her to replace her car when the time came. At the rate profits were going, she'd have the funds to purchase a much newer vehicle, especially if her current car held out another year. Wouldn't that be something?

Sharing a Beverage

I blame greed for the demise of our promising relationship. Mason enjoyed accusing me of greed. *Promising* was my mother's word on every available occasion to describe her thoughts about Mason and our future.

Mason preferred to get dinner together at restaurants with a drive-through window. We'd park in the lot and eat together facing the windshield. At first, I worried he didn't want to appear with me in public, but when he invited me to his cousin's wedding, he introduced me to everyone he knew. When we attended his annual work party, I received the same treatment. Soon after, though, he let a comment slip to reveal his opinion regarding tips. It occurred to me he could avoid giving a tip if we frequented restaurants without going inside.

Each time we ate out, Mason would suggest we share a beverage. The first time, I thought it romantic and endearing, but the second time, when I went to take a sip, I found the cup almost empty.

"You can have the rest," he said.

He commented with an air of generosity as if he were doing me a huge favor. The beverage was 90 percent consumed. I took a sip but left a bit at the bottom to wash everything down at the end of my meal. When I went for my drink, the cup was empty.

"I thought you said I could have the rest," I said. My thirst somehow bolstered my boldness.

"Greedy," he said.

Strike one for handsome Mason.

When he asked what types of things I'd enjoy doing with him, I let Mason know I preferred traditional dates like meals out, movies, concerts, or bowling. My tastes weren't extravagant, and Mason earned a senior engineer's wage. I was still finishing up my master's degree and living off a loan, so he always offered to pay. He had no school loans and no debt.

He even shared he'd been able to save enough to pay

for his luxury car outright, so I didn't worry our modest weekend activities would ruin him.

At the theater one afternoon, I warned him I liked popcorn with my movies, but he planned to rid me of that vice. Trying to pretend he'd forgotten, he led me by the elbow on an end-around arc as far from the counter as possible. I didn't plan to live a life where I couldn't eat popcorn at a movie, so I cleared my throat and raised my voice. "Let's get some popcorn. It can be my treat."

"Fine," he said. "Can we share a drink?"

I groaned but agreed.

True to form, before I'd even had a chance at a second gulp, the beverage disappeared. I should have called him greedy. When I whispered something about going out for more soda, he called me greedy. Strike two.

After giving it some thought, I decided frugality was not a deal-breaker trait. I suggested a free activity. We would drive to the nearby state park and hike the trails together for our next date. When we arrived, I realized I'd forgotten we would need a sticker to park on the grounds. The cost of an annual sticker is twenty-five dollars. I grew up in a family that valued state parks. My parents both invested in the stickers each year out of duty since we used the parks regularly.

I apologized to Mason for forgetting about the charge and not warning him. I couldn't volunteer to pay since I hadn't brought my wallet. Mason grew indignant about the cost. He turned his car around and found free street parking. Now we had an extra mile to walk on the shoulder of Highway M, an unpleasant place for pedestrians because of its high traffic and lack of sidewalks.

Mason grumbled about the parking fee and the audacity of the government to charge it. He applauded himself for getting around the system, while I imagined a future of risking our children's lives walking along the side of a busy highway to avoid paying for parking.

The next day, my mother served my favorite breakfast to me and slipped the word *promising* into our conversation as she mentioned the time Mason and I had been spending together.

"Mother, I know you think Mason is the guy for me, but I'll break it off with him as soon as I muster the courage. I'm struggling to figure out what words to use. He's just so darned frugal. It's annoying."

"Your father used to be frugal in his day too. Maybe it's an engineer thing. I helped him out of it. Don't let that stop you."

"Mother, I hate to disappoint, but I don't think he's the guy for me."

Whether I was ever in love with Mason, only the Lord knows. My mother puts great stock in genuine love. Remembering this, I attempted to smooth things over with her.

"Mother, I just don't think I'm in love with him," I said.

"Ah, well. There you go. I can't argue with that. When you're in love, you'll know it."

I rolled my eyes at her response since I knew she wasn't looking, but then I wondered who I was to argue with her concerning something I might know nothing about.

"That's okay. I'm over him already," she said. She held out her arms and snapped the fingers of both hands.

"My friend Marlene has a son who just moved back from Germany. He's single and a pharmacist. Pharmacists seem so stable. He may be just who you need to balance that adventuresome spirit of yours. What do you think? Should I call Marlene?"

Approachable

Molly gave a quick peek in the mirror before heading out for the day. Like her mother, she could go from waking to leaving the house in under twenty minutes. And that included a bowl of cereal.

Time is life. Molly had no interest in wasting her life doing her hair and putting on make-up. She hadn't been raised that way. After applying moisturizer and lip color, she was prepared to face the day. She didn't even own a curling iron or straightener. Wash and go was her preferred routine. With her naturally wavy hair, the result worked.

People would stop Molly to ask for directions. Once,

when she told her friends how often she was stopped for directions or asked to take a photo, her friends credited her with having an approachable look.

Molly figured she could do worse.

Another comment she heard often was, "Do I know you?"

She'd say, "I don't think so. I just have a common face."

Molly reminded people of their niece or a former co-worker. She heard it all the time. She didn't mind.

Later that day, while Molly ran errands, a child walked up to her in a store. The girl pulled on her sleeve to get her attention and asked for Molly's help. The young girl had been separated from her mother.

"Mommy says pick a lady with a friendly face. I'm Maisy. I'm four."

The girl held up four fingers. Molly smiled at her and offered her hand.

After the girl and her mother were reunited, Molly went home for the night. She took a satisfied look at herself in the mirror.

"Face, you did well today. Keep up the good work."

The New Floor

Dallas never knew when he might get a speeding ticket or need to stop for a train pulling a hundred cars. There was no way he was going to risk being late. He needed this job.

Until he knew how things worked under the new regime, he'd be extra careful. Dallas left home an extra half hour early. At his last place of employment, they had fired another guy when he arrived late to a job site twice in one month. Who knew what this new boss would do? He seemed strict about his policies. Anyway, Dallas wasn't the sort to gamble with job security to catch an extra fifteen minutes of sleep in the morning.

He drove past the worksite thirty minutes before the

hour. Dallas noticed opened blinds, so he figured the homeowner was awake. He drove around the block to get his bearings, then headed back to the convenience store he'd passed four minutes earlier. To be on the cautious side, Dallas used their restroom. He purchased a large diet soda with a screw-on cap. There'd be no chance of spillage. His tank was only down a quarter, but he filled his truck with gas and spent extra time cleaning his windshield and headlights.

Seven minutes before the hour, Dallas pulled up to the house. He took a quick snapshot of the home with his phone, including the address number in the picture he sent to his boss. Rather than punching a clock, he took photos at work sites every morning and forwarded them to his boss as required. In addition, the new protocol included a list of rules:

> Be on time. No excuses.
>
> Do not play music if the owner is home.
>
> Do not use the owner's restroom.
>
> Do not spill. All beverages must have a screw-on cap.
>
> Do not eat in client homes. At lunch, leave the premises or eat in your vehicle.

Dallas never knew who might answer the door. His favorite days were when the owners left home, and he worked in solitude. Today, an older woman greeted him before he even knocked. She introduced herself as Mrs. Morris as she walked him toward the rear of the home to show him the area that needed flooring.

"My husband promised to put a new floor in. He pulled up the old stuff, but he passed away last October."

"I'm sorry to hear that, ma'am."

"He kept promising me he'd get the floor in, but it never happened."

"Let's see if we can't get you your new floor today."

"My husband told me for three years he'd replace the floor. He got as far as removing what was there, and that was that. I never could get him to finish the project. Do you think you'll finish by the end of the week? How many days will it take?"

"If I don't run into troubles, I might finish by the end of the day."

The woman raised her eyebrows.

At noon, the young man picked up his work area a bit and headed for his truck. He thought he'd grab a sandwich and banana and use the station restroom while he was there.

"You're leaving before you've finished?" Mrs. Morris asked.

"Just out for a lunch break, Ma'am. I'll be back soon."

"I have leftover lasagna."

"Lasagna sounds great, but I was going to head to the station and pick up some lunch."

"Don't you like lasagna? I'd be happy to make you something else."

"I love lasagna, but I don't think my boss would approve. He likes us to eat in our trucks or off-site."

"It'll be our secret. If you won't tell, I won't. I'm not planning to hear another word about it. I hate throwing food away, and I haven't learned to cook for one yet. You're staying. The restroom is down the hall there. Help yourself."

The phone rang as soon as she served Dallas, and by the time Mrs. Morris finished her conversation, Dallas had cleared his dishes and was back at work.

At five o'clock, he carried a load of tools out to his truck. Mrs. Morris caught him at the front door as he returned.

"Give me the bad news. How many more days?"

"I'm finished. Go see."

"You have to be kidding."

He smiled, but she didn't return the smile. "Come back and have a peek," he said.

The two walked together to the back of the house, and he showed her the completed floor.

"I need to take a few pictures for my boss so he can see the work."

As Dallas took his pictures, the homeowner inspected

the floor. She paid close attention to the corners and the edges.

"I can't believe you finished this in one day. It looks beautiful. I've waited for a new floor for three years. My husband promised, but it just never got done."

"Yes, ma'am."

"If I'd known someone could finish the work in one day, I'd have called your company long ago. I should have scheduled the project for deer hunting season. My husband never missed deer hunting. The man sat outside in the cold for ten hours a day on a long weekend without a single complaint, but he couldn't find eight hours to work on the floor. He promised me he'd do it. That's the thing I can't get over. He promised."

"Yes, ma'am. I hope you don't mind. I need to finish these photos to send to my boss.

"You've done beautiful work. I love it. If I had known the job only took a day, I would have called your company long ago. The thing is, a person shouldn't promise to do something they don't plan to do. He shouldn't have promised."

The Journal

P age after page, his blue eyes look up at Christy from their photo album. His beautiful blue eyes. That smile.

He's gone now, though. Her key process for survival the past three weeks—except for the comfort she's found through friends and her children—has been writing in her journal.

After three weeks of recording wonderful memories and listing things about their life together for which she's thankful, its pages are full. She closes the photo album, places it back on the shelf, and picks up her phone to shop for a new journal.

The Jacket

Forecasts of the first snowfall of the year gave Bridget the motivation she needed to tackle her front closet. She pulled coats, gloves, jackets, and hats from the hangers and shelves and piled them in a heap on the nearby sofa. She should have wrestled with the task last spring, but today she forgave herself for her tendency to procrastinate and moved forward.

One by one, she sifted through each item, deciding to keep or give away. The task was best accomplished while the rest of her family was out of the house since half of them were reluctant to get rid of anything. Bridget had learned from experience to give when no one was looking.

Bridget hadn't noticed it as she emptied the closet, but when she picked up the new jacket with its $350 price tag still attached, she gasped. Oh no, Emma! Bridget didn't know if she could handle the stealing anymore. When Emma was younger, Bridget had driven her back to stores on more than a couple of occasions, requiring her to return stolen merchandise and apologize to a manager. But returning stolen items might not be as simple for a seventeen-year-old. One of these days, a store official would press charges, and Emma would be in trouble with the law.

Bridget made room for herself on the sofa among the family's winter things. She needed to come up with a plan. After several minutes, she stood up, grabbed her purse, and drove to the store identified on the jacket price tag. She filled a shopping cart with gift items. Combining her plan with Christmas shopping made sense. She may as well kill two birds with one large stone. Bridget loaded the cart with merchandise, checked out at a front register, and rushed home.

Her oldest daughter arrived home later that evening from drama practice. Bridget pulled Emma aside and confronted her about the coat. "It's not like you needed another jacket. You have more than enough."

Emma seemed contrite. Bridget couldn't bring herself to phone the police. She'd warned her daughter she'd phone the authorities if this situation ever happened again. Now, she couldn't follow through with it.

Caroline enjoyed her work at the upscale sporting goods shop. She found it easy to get excited about the camping and hiking merchandise. In fact, in the few months since she'd started, she'd risen to the top of the sales board. The store posted aspects of employee sales at the end of each week. Caroline had topped the list for the last four weeks straight.

Besides the work itself, Caroline enjoyed the people she worked with. Many of the employees loved hiking, biking, and camping as much as she did. She'd begun spending time with coworkers on her days off. Dark-haired Joshua in the bike department had talked to her, and she was eager to get to know him better.

Caroline knew the two of them were about the same age. Just like her, he had earned his undergraduate degree in English. Now he was working his way through law school at the local university. Caroline was applying to graduate schools and was hunting for work that would make use of her degree. She decided she would move forward with whichever option opened up first. That's how she would decide between career and graduate school.

In the meantime, she had her job at the outdoor store.

She didn't earn enough at the store to meet her living expenses, but it came close. Her parents helped her make ends meet by offering rent-free living. Caroline looked forward to moving back on her own, but she felt thankful for the help at the moment. And though it wasn't her dream job, she was thankful for the regular paycheck.

Bridget told Emma she'd call the store and pay for the jacket, but Emma would need to reimburse her the $350 out of the tips she earned from her weekend job. Emma promised to do as her mother instructed. She even created a chart to document the payments she planned to make, printed a copy, and taped it inside one of their kitchen cabinets. The next day she made her first payment of twenty dollars from money she'd been saving to purchase Christmas gifts.

Bridget called the store the next day and asked to speak to a manager. She explained to the manager she had purchased many items the day before, and the employee at the register had missed a jacket and not charged her for it.

"Yes, I have the receipt here in my hand, and it does not list the jacket," she said. "I'd like to take care of it over the phone if that's possible." Bridget spoke in a friendly tone, hoping not to arouse suspicion. The manager asked her if there was a security tag attached to the jacket.

Since there was not, she took payment from Bridget for the jacket with a credit card after answering several questions regarding information printed on her receipt. Had Emma learned how to remove security tags now?

Caroline arrived at work the following morning. After an hour at the register, an employee relieved her position and told her the store manager wanted to see her in her office. When Caroline reached the back office, her manager instructed her to sit down and handed her termination papers.

"We received a call yesterday. A woman you waited on the other day wasn't charged for a $350 jacket. Her receipt shows you served her at your register. Your name was on the receipt. The woman purchased about twenty items, but she noticed the black jacket when she got home. You even removed the security tag, but you never rang it up. We went over and over this in training. Even though it's your first recorded error, it's just too big of a mistake to ignore. We're going to let you go, Caroline."

Caroline found it difficult to respond. "You haven't even given me a warning or an opportunity to defend myself." She managed a few words before the manager cut her off, though she knew she might cry if she did much talking.

"Here's the paperwork. When you started, we explained it's our policy to hire and fire at will. If the error had been a few dollars, it might be different, but this is just too big of a mistake. We can't ignore it. Clear your locker. We'll mail you your paycheck. Security will escort you to the door."

Caroline collected her belongings from her locker and started the long walk from the back office, across the entire store floor, and out the front door. Keeping her eyes forward, she walked as fast as possible, all the while wondering if Joshua or any of her work friends were watching. She would be hard to miss with the security guy on her tail. Caroline held her tears back until she got to the parking lot, climbed in her car, and drove toward home.

After several days passed, Caroline contacted attorneys to make inquiries regarding the possibility of a wrongful termination suit. Her parents were on her side and urged her to find a lawyer. All three attorneys she contacted declined to move forward and take the case. Caroline still did not know how she missed a jacket. She always held on to a garment from the moment she removed a security tag until after she rang up an item. They emphasized this during training, so she took extra care to comply.

There had to be more to the story. She didn't know what happened. Being denied an opportunity to discuss the situation with the company frustrated her. There'd been no chance for her to defend herself. She fretted, worried, and lost sleep as she considered what she would do next with her life. Caroline had searched for a year after college graduation before she found this retail job. This blemish on her record would make job hunting even more difficult than before.

A Farmer's Retirement

For over sixty years, Delbert labored hard in his fields. At age eighty, he and his wife Anne leased their farmland and moved into town. Now they could sleep until eight o'clock if they wanted.

After lunch, they'd sit in their chairs, elevate their feet, and hold hands. Sometimes they'd take a quick nap.

"I don't miss all the work," he'd say. "No, sir! Not one bit."

After Anne passed on, Delbert fell and broke his hip. He moved into assisted living, but even once his hip healed, he remained.

"I worked hard all my life. Nice people take care of me here. I watch television, spend time with friends, and I never eat alone anymore. This is the life."

Four Lakes Pottery Studio

An angry customer phoned to check on her pottery piece for the second time that week. She'd expected her dish to be glazed and ready for pickup ten days earlier, but neither of the clerks she talked to could find it on the shelves designated for completed pottery.

A Girl Scout troop had just left, so the shop was empty for a moment. The customer was shouting through the phone into Elizabeth's ear. She put it on speaker to allow her employee Melissa to hear too.

"You said it'd be ready by now. Why isn't it ready? The woman who checked me out was in her mid-twenties with light brown hair. Shoulder length. She promised me it would be ready for pickup in ten days."

Elizabeth wanted to respond that no one by that description worked at the studio, but she sucked her lips in and held them in place with her teeth. Sometimes it was best to let a customer vent.

The shop owner, Elizabeth, was thirty years old with blonde hair. Melissa was forty-two with dark brown hair. None of the women who worked in the shop were in their mid-twenties.

The other two employees were over fifty, plus there was Adam, who subbed whenever someone took time off.

Melissa headed to the back room to prepare for an afternoon birthday party. Twelve seven-year-olds were due to arrive soon. Elizabeth jotted down the disgruntled customer's name and number and promised to call her back that day. She hunted in the system with no luck.

Because one of the older employees was new and had made a couple of mistakes that week, Elizabeth checked all the pieces unloaded from the kiln that were waiting for her to tidy up with the Dremel. She examined all the pieces her co-worker Dremel polished but hadn't yet matched up with the client's paperwork. She fetched the step stool and looked at the bottom of each unclaimed-after-three-months piece on the shelf above the register in case the new employee had made a mistake.

Forty-two-year-old Melissa pulled the skin on both sides of her face and neck taut, raised her eyebrows, and said, "Do you think she means me?" The two of them laughed.

Elizabeth said, "Do you think she meant me? Could my hair pass for brown?"

"It couldn't even pass for dishwater blonde, but nice try."

After several hours of searching in between working with clients, Elizabeth took a deep breath and phoned the angry woman back. She didn't recognize the area code, but with cell phones these days, that might mean nothing.

Elizabeth apologized when the woman answered the phone. Again, the customer described the young woman who served her. She said the studio employee promised her piece would be completed before three o'clock.

Elizabeth's shop never promised pieces at a particular time. Pottery was ready by 9:00 a.m. when the shop opened or ready on another day.

"Did you mean to call the Four Lakes Pottery Studio in Madison, Wisconsin? I'm searching, and I notice there's a shop with the same name in the state of Washington.

"Oh, good grief! No wonder you never called me!" The woman from Washington hung up on Elizabeth, saying nothing else and without apologizing.

Melissa pulled the sides of her face back and looked at the mirror on the wall near the sink. "Come on. Tell me the truth. I look twenty-eight, don't I?"

Elizabeth faced Melissa and rolled her eyes. "Without a doubt!" They both broke into a laugh.

The Piano Teacher

During each lesson, Mrs. Beck asks her students how their practice went that week. After thirty years of teaching piano, she doesn't need to ask, but students don't know this. She can often tell by their posture before they play a single note on the piano. Well-prepared students walk in with a confidence that unprepared students lack.

Every time she asks, Max says he's had a good practice week. Sometimes he's telling the truth. Sometimes he isn't. Most of her students are more honest than Max, but she still loves him in spite of this fault. The students who have been with her longest are her favorites, but she would never admit this out loud.

Anna tries to be honest, but she's too young to remember practice details. She often says she might not have practiced the expected number of days, but her mother confirms she's done the work when Anna and Mrs. Beck check in with Anna's mom after her lesson.

Mrs. Beck knows the promise of a piece of candy at the end of each lesson drives Sam to practice. He always comes well-prepared. Mrs. Beck is careful to have Sam's favorite candy brands in stock.

Four of the students she's taught the longest call her Mrs. Beck. She loves this because it reminds her of her former days when she directed the local high school choirs. Her choir students all called her Mrs. Beck. When she taught in the public high school, that's how things were done.

Some of the young mothers of her private students now instruct their children to call her Miss Isabella. She isn't fond of the trend. Isn't Mrs. Beck easier to say than Miss Isabella? She hasn't been a miss for thirty-three years. She's proud to be Mrs. Beck, but she also values respect. And she respects the young mothers enough to go along with whatever ridiculous name they tell their children to call her.

Some of her private students call her by her first name when they grow older. She can't imagine ever calling one of her teachers by their first name, especially without an invitation, but she knows times are different.

Different doesn't mean better, but she wouldn't dream of correcting them.

A few years ago, Noah asked what he should call her. She answered that she'd prefer Mrs. Beck because it reminded her of wonderful days as a choral director. She told him he could call her Isabella if he preferred, but he's always called her Mrs. Beck, and because of that, he has a special place in her heart.

When she started teaching, she was younger than the parents of most of her students. Then, for a time, she was about the same age. Now she's older than all the parents. She enjoys watching the young families. Sometimes it's the dad or a nanny who brings the student, but usually, it's the moms, even though most of them work outside the home too.

She hears so many negative comments in the news about young people.

If only the world could see the younger generations—both her students and their parents—through her eyes. How encouraged they'd be. Her students come to lessons with manners. They're well-dressed and clean. And they've trimmed their nails, which is important with piano.

Moms somehow get the students to their lessons on time and pick them up on time. She doesn't know how they do it. Most are so busy.

Almost all of her students thank her at least once or twice at the end of their lesson. She wonders if she ever remembered to thank her piano teacher when she was young. She hopes she did. Even though Mrs. Villmer passed away ten years ago, she feels a pang now and then because she didn't realize what a terrific teacher she had when she was a child. It's too late now to send her a note of appreciation.

Mrs. Beck enjoys sending her piano students and their parents notes in the mail. There's so much to commend— she can always think of something to say to encourage young players and their parents. It must be much more difficult to raise children now with all the technical devices they have access to. What kid would choose to put their video game down to practice piano? And yet, they often do just that.

Sometimes the parents wait in the lounge at the music school during lessons. Mrs. Beck notices the mothers helping younger siblings with their homework while they wait. The younger siblings seldom argue or run around or scream or hit each other. They speak in hushed tones and almost always remember to pick up their mess before they leave.

A few of her students share the candy they earn with their younger siblings, even though she's never heard the parents instruct them to do so. Mrs. Beck marvels at this.

She can't imagine ever sharing candy with her younger sister without being forced. Of course, back when she took piano lessons, teachers didn't offer candy. Teachers expected students to do the work without candy in those days. But the world is different now. It's amazing the power one or two pieces of candy have to inspire practice.

The Diary

When Alyssa noticed the time, she dropped her pen and leaped off her bed. "Bye, Mom!" The door slammed behind her.

The single mother headed to Alyssa's room to gather laundry. She paused and her jaw dropped when she noticed angry words on an open diary page.

I hate my mom!!! She's the absolute worst!!!

One minute before curfew, Alyssa returned home smiling and humming.

"Did you girls enjoy the movie?"

"It was decent. Sorry about the crazy fit I threw earlier."

"Thank you for apologizing. I'm growing accustomed to adolescent drama. Who needs movies with a teenager in the house? Good night, sweetie."

"Night. Love you, Mom."

The Phone Call

"Could you pass the ketchup, dear?" Holly's husband asked. Before she could stop her train of thought long enough to respond and slide the ketchup down the table, he added, "Did you call the flooring place today?"

"No," Holly said. She had meant to call, but she forgot again for the third day in a row. She felt her jaw clench. "I'll try to remember to do it tomorrow. It's been a hectic week."

"Okay," he said.

You have no idea how busy my day was, Holly thought. What's the big hurry with the flooring anyway? We ordered it. They said they'd call when it was time to install. They said at least three weeks, and it's only been four. What's the big hurry?

Holly felt a strong urge to run away right then. Nothing permanent. Maybe a long browsing session at the bookstore. Maybe a double feature. She'd always dreamed of seeing a double feature, but life seemed so hectic all the time. She hadn't seen a movie all year. Not one. And she loved movies. Two movies in a row all by herself would be a nice break.

Husbands! It isn't husbands so much as it is their bossiness. She hated phone calls. They put you on hold, made you wait fifteen minutes. Sometimes thirty. Who had the time? She hated phone calls! Why do I need to make all the calls anyway? Just because he works so darned much? What's the point? I'm starting to wonder. Where's a good cliff when you need one? Wait. Hold on. Don't get carried away, Holly. But really! If I can't have a bit more lead on this collar, I'm going to suffocate.

"What's wrong, dear?" her husband asked. "Everything okay? Here, let me grab the ketchup. I only asked because you were closer. It's no big deal." He stood and walked over to get the ketchup, squeezing her shoulder as he passed by in a rare affectionate gesture.

"Are you feeling okay?" he asked her.

"I'm fine. Why?"

"It's just that you look overheated, and the look on your face."

Holly burst into tears. "Nothing is wrong. Just these hot flashes again. It's been a bad week for them. I'll call about the floor tomorrow. I'm sorry."

"Forget about it." He shrugged. "It's no big deal. I'll call the place tomorrow. I just want to make sure they haven't forgotten about us since we gave them our money." He continued, "After dinner, I'll clean up here, and you go read or take a bath or something. With the kids away at school now, your schedule should lighten up a bit, shouldn't it?"

"Maybe I don't want it to lighten up. I liked being a mother." Holly let out a little sob. "And why haven't they called? This growing up and moving away stuff stinks!"

"You're still their mother. The twins will always need you. But maybe a calmer life around here will be nice, though. Just the two of us feels good too, doesn't it? How about a movie this weekend? I'll spring for popcorn and the works. We can even sit in one of those recliner love-seats together."

Holly pulled a tissue from her pocket, wiped the sweat from her forehead, and then wiped her nose.

"And if we haven't heard from the kids by Sunday, we'll track 'em down," he said.

"Could you pass the ketchup back? I never got any."

Her husband stood up, walked over, and handed her the ketchup. He patted her on the back and smiled.

He's awfully handsome when he smiles, Holly thought.

"Thanks, dear," she said, and she offered him her own tired smile. After a few moments, she added, "A movie and a bucket of popcorn sounds like a dream. I may take you up on your offer to load the dishwasher tonight too."

The Interrogation Consistency

Friends and family asked why she would quit her job in the States to move across the world where she didn't know a soul. Kara told everyone it was for the adventure. In part, she spoke the truth. She loved adventure, but the real reason Kara quit her job—a successful position for a growing computer software company—was to flee the pain of a broken relationship. Her boyfriend of three years ended things between them, and it devastated her.

Kara couldn't face the questions of well-meaning friends and acquaintances. How could she grieve the loss of the man she loved when someone mentioned his name to her every day? She gave notice at the job she adored and traveled alone from her home in the Midwest to the Asian country of Nepal.

After landing at the airport in Kathmandu, Kara rode in a tiny cab to her designated training location. Because of her height, she found it necessary to hunch over in the back seat the entire ride. She held her hands over her head to shield it, hoping to avoid a concussion as she and the driver traveled the bumpy roads. As she crouched in the rear of the small vehicle, she recalled a discussion with her mother three weeks earlier.

"Forgive my tone, but you cannot be serious. If you tried, I'm quite certain you could find a place to run to that's closer to home than Nepal. You don't know a soul there. I'll worry myself sick. How about Disney World? Or Yellowstone?

"It'll be okay, Mom. I'm only going for a few months. I need to clear my head. And I've always dreamed of seeing Mount Everest. You know that. I'll be checking off two or three bucket-list items with one plane ticket."

"One open-ended plane ticket. I'd feel so much better if you had a return date planned or if you knew some-one in Nepal. You don't know the language. You've never even been there before, Kara!"

"That's the point. I want to add another country to my list. It'll be okay. I've learned a few essential phrases, and you know how fast I can pick things up. There'll be other English-speaking teachers at the school too. I'll get to know them. In case I fall in love with the place, I want to leave my options open. That way, I'll have freedom to decide once I'm there."

Kara enjoyed the two days of sightseeing in Kathmandu sponsored by the agency. The director of the organization served as a guide. After forty-eight hours of team-building tourism, her official training started. With her affinity for languages, Kara picked up a number of common Nepali phrases.

Then, just two weeks later, with training completed, Kara and another teacher loaded themselves and their bags on a bus and headed toward their new home in Parbatipur. Remote was the term the director used. Kara only knew she loved the scenery as she gazed out the bus window. She loved the view of the mountain range in the distance. To the depths of her bones, she felt the relief of being half a world away from Jake, breaker-of-hearts.

Shannon, a twenty-year-old college student from Vancouver and six years younger than Kara, was on a year-long break from university to teach in Nepal. The two now shared a bedroom on the second floor in the home of their host family. The house was on the main street in the town above an office space owned and rented by the family.

At dinner the first night, Kara found, to her great pleasure, she could converse with her host, *Didi* (older sister). Didi knew some English. Combined with gestures and the Nepali Kara had picked up, they communicated while Shannon sat dumb-founded until Kara translated the Nepali parts for her. Didi's questions came fast.

Where are you from?

What is your age?

What is your husband's name?

You are not married?

You are twenty-six and not married?

Why aren't you married?

We will invite my nephew over for dinner. He is not married either.

The next day, Kara took a walk down the main street with Shannon. As the only white people in town, they received attention at almost every house and in front of many of the shops. People approached them in a friendly manner. They asked the young women the same questions over and over.

Hello. What is your name?

Where are you from?

What is your age?

Are you married?

You have no husband?

You are not married?

You are twenty-six and not married?

Why aren't you married?

Whether she and Shannon were walking down the street or biking, children of all ages would stop and greet the two white women. Kara felt as if all eyes were on her every moment. Shannon stood a mere five-foot-two inches tall and wore her brunette hair in a bob. Kara's height and blonde hair drew even more attention than Shannon received. Spectacle was the word for it. At five-foot-ten inches with long blonde hair, Kara was a spectacle.

Kids ran up to her: Chocolate? Chocolate? Do you have any chocolate?

Children rode their bikes and stopped in front of her with a greeting: Hello. What is your name? Where are you from? Australia? Are you married? Why not? How old are you?

With her passion for travel, the young woman was not new to being alone internationally, but she had never been asked if she was from Australia before. Germany, Norway, and Sweden, but never Australia. And she had never been questioned about her marital status so often either.

What is your father's name?

Are you married?

Do you have any sisters or brothers?

Is your sister married? How old is she?

The older ladies of the small Nepali town often gathered on porches in the afternoon to visit. As Kara walked home after teaching at the English school, the women she passed would flag her down.

Namaste, namaste, *bahini* (younger sister).

You're pretty.

Hello, what is your name?

Are you married?

How old are you?

See that man over there? See? Handsome. And I have a son who is not married.

One evening, after almost four months in the country, Kara was in the upstairs bathroom, taking a quick shower. Young girls at the school loved to touch and style her blonde hair with their unwashed hands during outdoor recess. This was her first shower in a week. Water warmed by the sun and pumped by the generator from her host family's well ran over her body. The sun had been out all day, so the water felt refreshing and warm. The warmest shower she'd enjoyed in a while. She was eager to experience the feel of clean hair again.

Kara decided there under the cascade of water that she was ready to return to her family. She knew her time in Nepal had prepared her to face the questions that would come her way back in the States. Nepal had brought daily rehearsals.

Are you married? Why not?

She'd answered those two phrases dozens of times here. The questions and their intent no longer held their power to crush. And besides, she was eager to return home where she could take a warm shower every day if she chose. What a luxury that would be.

One Hundred Years from Now

During a Sunday sermon, Jolene's pastor said, "One hundred years from now, no one on earth will remember anyone in this room." The statement hit her hard. She couldn't bear the thought that no one would remember her or her parents or her siblings. Her pastor meant to encourage the congregation to live purposeful lives, but Jolene accepted his words as a challenge and resolved to disprove his assertion.

After the church service, Jolene purchased a lavender three-ring binder. She secured a clear plastic envelope to its back. Every funeral or memorial card she'd collected over the years went into the envelope.

Jolene searched for the names of relatives, friends,

neighbors, and classmates. She hunted online for their obituaries, printed them out, and organized them alphabetically in the binder. She remembered former employers, schoolteachers, and her parents' friends.

For years, Jolene's mother had clipped obituaries and mailed them to her. Jolene located those now and affixed a second plastic envelope to a second binder. Soon several purple binders housed the names and obituaries of hundreds of people Jolene wanted to remember. She organized them with relatives in one, friends in another, and so on.

As a prolific author, Jolene expects some of her words will hold meaning powerful enough to rupture the truth of her pastor's statement. She names her characters after deceased family and friends to bring them honor. She wants their names remembered alongside hers.

Every year on Memorial Day, Jolene devotes hours to paging through her lavender binders, remembering with thankfulness those who've impacted her life. She's blessed to have known many wonderful people during her lifetime, and she's determined she'll not forget them.

On her seventieth birthday, Jolene decides to leave the binders to her oldest niece. While Crystal is not her favorite, she is the niece who traveled with her to The Tower of London, Lincoln's tomb, and Flannery O'Connor's childhood home. Crystal is the family member who cares enough about history to value the binders and the information they contain. She even studied history in college. And she's her only relative who will visit cemeteries with her on Memorial Day to place flowers on the graves of family members. Jolene trusts Crystal will remember when she no longer can.

Vacationing in Seattle

Following the bustle of Pike Place Market and the beauty of Chihuly Garden and Glass, the couple savored a salmon dinner while seated at a table overlooking scenic Lake Union.

They strolled the boardwalk after dessert, reading details on "yacht for sale" signs, imagining aloud life together on a houseboat.

The wife directed her husband's attention to the couple strolling ahead of them, asking if he noticed the stream of toilet paper trailing from the woman's waistband. He nodded.

"Now, there's a husband who doesn't care about his wife," she said in a hushed tone.

"Why do you say that?"

"He had to have seen it. He followed her for a while. I've been watching. He sees, but he's not saying anything. Where's the love in that?"

A Gardening Life

Mrs. Turney scuttled across her side lawn and up the slope to our front porch. I noticed her approaching as I looked out our side window. Before she rang our doorbell, I opened the door and greeted her. With quick words and a welcoming gesture, she invited me to come next door.

Her garage doors were open, and as I stepped in, I could see dozens of loaves of bread on display on tall metal racks. To the right, on the clean garage floor, two enormous tubs overflowed with large onions.

"Take whatever you want," she said in her rushed manner. She motioned with her arms in a commanding way that made it impossible for me to refuse. I was to take whatever I wanted of the bread and onions. She handed me a brown paper bag. When I chose just one loaf of bread, she exhorted me to take some more. "You can freeze it. You have a family. Take more if you'll use it. I have all I can use and then some."

I filled my bag with the brand of bread our family ate every week. Satisfied, she turned my attention to the onions. "Onions grow in abundance on my son's farm," Mrs. Turney said. "Whatever the neighbors don't want will be fed to the cows." She handed me a plastic bag when I took two of the onions.

"Take more. They last for months if you keep them in the produce drawer of your refrigerator."

They were huge, gorgeous onions. As I filled my bag, she shuffled around, rearranging bread, filling the empty spots, moving much faster than an average woman of eighty-five years. When my bags were full, I thanked her.

As I headed home, she scurried down to the end of her driveway, putting her open hand above her eyes to shield them from the sun. I realized she was looking for people she knew as they drove past in order to wave them into her driveway. Before I made it to my door, a neighbor had pulled over and was walking up her driveway to shop for bread and onions. A few seconds later, another car pulled over. It seemed the neighbors knew the drill.

This was the first of many times she invited me over for bread. Once or twice a month, an admirer of hers delivered day-old loaves to her home. The man owned a bread and bakery shop in the nearby town of Middleton. Another neighbor soon filled me in. The owner of the bread store attended the same church as Mrs. Turney. He was a widower with a long-time crush on her. The man had proposed to Mrs. Turney more than once, but she had no interest in marrying again. She seemed to delight in having an admirer, though.

Mrs. Turney's male friend permitted her to distribute the surplus as she saw fit. On nice weather days, she took walks around the block, filled paper bags in hand, offering loaves to any neighbor who was outside.

On "bread day," Mrs. Turney was at her height of popularity. Her face would light up and glow with the social interaction.

About a year after the first time she invited me over for bread, she came and knocked on my door. "Rosie's in Florida this week. Would you like to walk around the block with me? I've seen you take walks around this time before." Rosie was my other widowed next-door neighbor.

As we walked, I didn't need to slow myself down to keep in step with my senior neighbor. She was full of energy. Mrs. Turney told me her husband used to farm all the land that now held our neighborhood. Her home used to be down the road five houses and across the street, about where a pink-sided house stands now. They had torn her home down when her son developed the land. Her old home had been set back a bit from the road, and behind it she had an immense garden. She grew potatoes, tomatoes, beans, corn, strawberries, raspberries, lettuce, green peppers, and peas. In addition, she had three patches of rhubarb. Mrs. Turney had raised six children on food from that garden and was proud of it.

"I used to can enough tomato juice to last the year. I canned, and I froze. We had a huge freezer in the kitchen. I still have one, so when the grandkids stop by for lunch, I can always grab something and cook for them."

A woman on the other side of the block was out in her front yard weeding. As we walked by, Mrs. Turney said hello in a friendly manner, but we kept walking. "I know that woman, but I can't think of her name," she said. "I mean, I know her very well. Her son used to play with my son Danny. He'd be over at our house all the time. And they go to our church. It's embarrassing—I mean, I know her. I'm just not good with names anymore."

When we were about a block from home, she said, "Did I tell you about my garden? I used to have a garden up there behind our house. It was huge. Two or three acres. I grew potatoes, tomatoes, beans, corn, strawberries, raspberries, lettuce, green peppers, and peas." She tallied the produce on her fingers as she talked. "I also had three patches of rhubarb." She held up three fingers. "We raised six children on food from that garden. I canned and I canned and I froze, and the food lasted all year. We had a huge freezer off the kitchen. Well, here we are. Thanks for walking with me. Would you like to see my house?" she asked. "Have you seen it before? My son built it when he developed the farmland."

Yes, I had seen it before. The week we moved in, she had invited me over for a tour. But she was proud of her home, and it was fresh for her every time she showed me. It was a beautiful house with a grand kitchen, so I enjoyed looking at it every time.

"Sure, I have a few minutes to see your home. I'd love a tour. Thanks."

We started in her kitchen. Behind the kitchen was a large pantry with an abundance of shelving and a freezer. She said, "I still do some canning now, and I freeze some things, but not what I used to do back when the kids were growing up. Have I told you about my garden?"

Axel Zwart

Axel Zwart's homeroom teacher, Miss Coomer, loves excusing her fourth-grade class alphabetically. Amy Acker always leads the class in line. Axel Zwart brings up the rear. One time the lunchroom ran out of chicken tenders by the time they got to the *W*'s. They served Axel a cold cheese sandwich. He hates cheese.

Another day, Axel missed the bus because Miss Coomer dismisses her students one at a time. She got worked up lecturing the always-misbehaving Noah Van Dyke and forgot all about the clock and the bus schedule.

Last month, Amy Acker's mother brought in cupcakes for the entire class in honor of Amy's birthday. Miss

Coomer called out her students' names to invite them to the front of the room to choose a cupcake.

"Let's go by alphabet. That way, we will serve the birthday girl first. As soon as Amy takes her first bite, the rest of you may join in," she said.

I think Miss Coomer intended for Amy to wait until she served everyone, but by the time Sean Hope held his cupcake in his hand, Amy's was in her belly. By the time Axel heard his name called, no cupcakes remained. Miss Coomer missed out too.

"Amy's mother must have misunderstood the count I gave her," she said. "Does anyone have half they're willing to share with Axel?" No one raised their hand. They were too busy licking their fingers and picking crumbs off their desks.

"Next time, I'll try to remember to start at the end of the alphabet. Sorry, Axel." Miss Coomer always seemed to forget to follow through with that promise, though.

The name Zwart comes in handy in gym class. That's about the only time. Axel hates gym and dreads the skill tests. On skill test days, he's called last, of course. The other students are on to the next thing by the time his turn comes around, so he has the good fortune of avoiding an audience. None of his classmates care enough to watch all the way to the end of the alphabet. Not like they do for the first students in line.

Last Wednesday in gym, the fourth-grade class took

part in the mile-run challenge. The physical education teacher sent students out in groups of six. Axel found himself in the last group.

The first group lined up six abreast in the six lanes of the nearby high school track. They started running when the gym teacher, stopwatch in hand, brought his arm down and shouted, "Go." Six minutes after the first group began, he blew the whistle for the next group, and so on. Only two students remained when it was time for the last group. Axel and Noah Van Dyke, who was the fastest kid in the class.

Noah and Axel started in lanes one and two, but Noah shot out in front. Axel was still on his third lap around the track as Noah crossed the finish line. The students who ran earlier lounged around on the grass, recovering and watching the others finish. Soon, Noah joined the rest of the class on the center grass. Axel was the lone runner on the track. The entire world watched him suffer his last lap.

To make matters worse, the teacher, intending to be nice, sent one of the fast kids from the first group out again to run with Axel, so he didn't have to finish alone. Max ran backward, keeping pace with Axel.

Two girls came up to him later. "Aw. Good job, Axel. Way to go." The pity in their voices only compounded his embarrassment.

After the mile-run challenge, Axel dreamed of

changing his surname to a middle-of-the-alphabet moniker like Miller or Nelson. Fate held him resolutely in its grip, though. Once a Zwart, always a Zwart.

The Envelope

Kathryn Chadwick and her husband kept a tidy yard, but the early snowfall caught them by surprise last autumn. They'd been unable to clear the leaves from their flower bed because the first snowfall stayed on the ground from early November through March.

Kathryn took advantage of the warm April vacation day to clear their lawn. She started on the northwest side, attacking it first since it was most visible to neighbors.

She bent down and cleared the bottom of each of the Knock Out rose bushes with her hands. Afterward, she'd blow the leaves to the curb. If that didn't work, she'd rake them up. Her husband was primary leaf raker of the household, but since he was out of the country for business, she'd handle the task. She didn't want to wait longer.

When she got to the fourth rose bush, she discovered a muddy, business-sized envelope. She took a break and went inside to clean it off with a dry cloth. The address on the envelope belonged to a neighbor on the other end of the street. Kathryn left it on her counter to dry off, then resumed her outdoor work.

Finished with the front, she left the beds in the backyard for her husband. Kathryn washed up, walked a block up the street, and knocked on the neighbor's door. She'd never met the woman before and didn't recognize her when she answered the door.

"Hi. I'm your neighbor from down the street. I live on this same side at 4332. I was clearing leaves from my shrubs and found this mail caught at the base of one of my plants." Kathryn handed it to the woman.

The woman took the envelope in her hands and said, "Oh, my gosh! This explains a lot."

"It must have got caught in the wind. It blew quite a ways down," said Kathryn.

"Oh my gosh! I cannot believe this." She opened the envelope and removed a check. "He said he sent it, but I didn't believe it. I didn't believe him! I was so nasty."

Looking as if she remembered the woman at the door was a stranger, she put the check back into the envelope and put her hands down at her sides. "Thanks so much for taking the trouble to walk up the street and deliver this to me. If only it had come last November." She said thanks one more time and began to shut the door as Kathryn stood there hoping for more details.

Before it closed all the way, Kathryn said, "Sure. You're welcome."

Disappointed that she might never have answers to her questions, Kathryn turned back toward her home. She imagined the possibilities. What might the check have been? Who sent it? She couldn't wait to get home and call Roselyn. Roselyn knew everyone. If anyone could answer her questions, it was her neighbor Roselyn.

The Recuperation

Each day Tara gets more behind. She hasn't regained her strength yet. Tara realizes she returned to work too soon, but there's nothing to do about it now. By the end of the day, she barely has the energy to get home and change out of her clothes for bed.

She knows she should do laundry, but the baskets are full of dirty clothes, and it's hard to sort laundry without baskets. The clothing in the dryer is too wrinkled to wear. It's been sitting in there for a while. She should re-wash it, but the washing machine is full of towels waiting to go into the dryer.

In the kitchen, the sink is full of dirty dishes she should wash. She could put them in the dishwasher, but it broke last week mid-cycle. The repair company said they'd send somebody out next Monday, but she and her husband Rick both work Monday, so Tara realizes she'll need to reschedule the appointment. It's the busy time of year at work for both of them, so they may need to delay repairs a month or two.

Tara planned that the two of them would work on the dishes last night, but her husband learned he had a two-hour call with a client in Hong Kong at the last minute. Tara was tired and overwhelmed. She sat and did nothing for an hour. Afterward, she called her sister and spent almost an hour venting about all she needed to do but didn't have the strength to accomplish.

Rick used his sick days to be with her when she was ill. His job is the demanding sort that leaves little surplus in the day for luxuries such as laundry or cooking. He thinks they should order dinners to be delivered and hire a maid service, at least until Tara feels like herself again. Tara says maids will clean, but homeowners need to prepare the home first by picking up. She says they are nowhere near having the house in good enough shape to hire a maid service.

Tara's sister advised her to focus on one thing at a time. Just do one thing. Tara said there are too many things. She confessed she might need someone to help her get started because it's too overwhelming.

The kitchen table is full of papers that need to be

organized so a bill doesn't get thrown away. Tara wonders aloud if it wouldn't be better to have lived in the days of Laura Ingalls Wilder before junk mail began its reign. She knows there's a wedding invitation floating somewhere among the papers on the counter, but the clutter is too overwhelming. She would call the people to RSVP, but she can't remember who is getting married.

Tara's friend Janice offered to help the other day when she heard Tara groaning about all there was to do, but Tara would rather live in a mess for eternity than allow Janice to bear witness to it. Janice keeps her own house organized and sparkling clean. Tara says she would die of embarrassment if Janice walked in her front door.

Three hours after her husband's two-hour phone call began, he hung up, then poured them each a bowl of cereal. When he opened the refrigerator, he discovered they only had milk enough for one, so he added the milk to Tara's bowl, served her, and ate his dinner of dry cereal as they sat next to each other on the sofa.

Tara shed tears as she finished her cereal. Her husband told her everything was going to be okay. "The most important thing is that you're feeling better. The doctor says you'll make a complete recovery, but it may take a while. We'll need to figure something out, but it's going to be okay. I wish you'd let me call someone."

"It's too embarrassing!"

"I have to go in to work on Saturday morning, but in

the afternoon, I'll tackle the kitchen and the laundry. We only need to survive until the weekend. The doctor says you're to rest in the evenings, so don't even think about helping. We need you to get better. It's our number one priority. The good news is I have enough shirts and underwear to make it until Saturday. Do you?"

Tara shrugged. She didn't know and didn't have the strength to care.

The next morning, the two headed for work at seven o'clock, and by eight o'clock, Tara's sister was making use of her key to their house. Remembering Tara's complaints, she'd brought along several empty clothes baskets, her Bluetooth speaker, and necessary cleaning supplies, including clean kitchen towels and dishcloths.

Rachel cleared enough counter space for her speaker and started listening to a new book while doing her work. She unloaded the washing machine and started the laundry process by re-washing the wrinkled clothes sitting in the dryer. While she waited for the washer and dryer cycles, she emptied the kitchen sink, cleaned it, and washed, dried, and put away the dishes.

By the time Rachel washed and dried the first load of clothing, she'd cleared the kitchen table off so she could use it to fold laundry. By one o'clock, she'd finished the dishes and cleaned the kitchen. Rachel sat down to enjoy the lunch she'd brought with her, and then she started on the floors, stopping every once in a while to switch loads of laundry, fold clothes, and put them away. By four o'clock, she was exhausted. She wrote a note to Tara and left it on the table for them.

Dear Tara,

My boss let me have the day off today. Please take Rick's advice now and call a maid service. I've done some research. If you look at the back side of this note, you'll find five services I recommend based on ratings and reviews.

You are loved, and I'm happy you're on the mend!

Your sister

P.S. I got Eddie's to deliver a chicken dish and a fruit tray this afternoon. I've ordered the chicken before—it's delicious! Look in the fridge. Heat covered at 325–350 for about an hour. You'll love it.

In the Library

A deadline drove me from home and my distracting to-do list to the quiet room of the local library. My favorite corner desk along the back wall stood available. Good fortune smiled on me. I took my coat off, and in less than two minutes, I'd organized my little writing station.

Once I settled into a working state of mind, a patron asked the desk clerk a question. The patron's voice operated at near full volume. Leaving the desk, the woman found a seat at a table and held a one-sided conversation with the person next to her.

After several minutes, I leaned out from my mini-cubicle and noticed two others at a table near her rolling their eyes in a mocking gesture. I heard several throats clear. It seemed everyone in the large room noticed except the offending woman. Headphones went on here and there, but I realized with deep sadness that I'd left mine at home.

I weighed my to-do list at home against the woman's voice, now as annoying as the buzz of a thousand mosquitoes. I looked at the time on my phone and gave the woman ten minutes. My deadline wasn't going anywhere. If she didn't quiet down, I'd have to head out. I thought to chasten her behavior with the glare my children have grown to despise, but a glare does no good without a recipient. My eyes could not catch her attention as I stood up and walked past her toward the fountain for a drink. I was no more successful on my return journey.

After ten minutes, the sound of her voice droned on. With wistful regret, I shoved my belongings into my bag and headed home. Thoughts of the selfish woman raced through my mind alongside schemes for avoiding my to-do list. I needed to be firm with myself. To meet my deadline, my list would need to take a brief vacation.

Learning to Drive

Christine's right foot stomped the floorboard to stop the car. Her anxiety mounted as she sat in the front passenger seat of her own vehicle. Experience did not ease her symptoms. Her upset stomach, sweaty hands, and rapid heartbeat grew worse each time. Her eighteen-year-old daughter sat behind the wheel, training for her driver's license. Christine decided she would never have what it takes for this task.

One evening later that week, she almost exploded from the stress. She snapped at her daughter to pull to the side of the road. Chloe's shoulders drooped. She pulled the car over, and they switched places. Less than three minutes afterward, they came to a traffic backup. After several minutes without moving, watching emergency vehicles pass along the right shoulder, the mood in the car shifted.

"Mom. It's just like Brittney. This is close to the spot too. My hands are shaking. Look at them." The line of cars stood still, so Christine put the car in park. She reached over and took her daughter's hands in hers. Holding them, she kept her eyes on the road as she bent over and kissed her daughter's hands.

Brittney and Chloe had been best friends. They attended different schools but competed on the same city swim team and showed horses in 4-H Club together. One snowy night while driving home from her new job at the mall, Brittney's car slipped on the ice, crossing the center line. The accident killed her on impact.

After Brittney's death, Chloe had no interest in learning to drive. She'd been in no hurry. But now that she was headed to college, she decided getting her license was an important step toward moving ahead with her life.

Chloe planned to attend the University of Wisconsin in Milwaukee in the fall. She'd be able to drive to college if she got her license. She'd be free to make the ninety-minute trip home to visit on weekends whenever she desired. Her dad offered to hand his car down to her. All that was missing was a driver's license. The time had come.

"I think my fears are interfering with your ability to drive," Christine said as they waited for the road to open up again. "You're better than I'm allowing you to be. Maybe you're a lot better. I'm sorry. I'm your mom, and I don't know any other way to be. I have an idea, though. Let's have your dad teach you."

"He's too busy, Mom."

"He'll be home this weekend, and we have nothing planned," Christine said. "I talked to him about taking Monday off since school is closed. Somehow, he could make it work. If you focus on driving all three days, you'll have your required hours in. All you'll need to do is take the test."

"I'll try it if you're sure Dad is willing. I can't believe he's taking Monday off. The last time he took a day off for no reason—well, there has never been a time. Has there, Mom?"

"Not for a while."

On Saturday, Chloe and her dad were ready to go by eight o'clock in the morning. They drove around town for about fifteen minutes. Bill suggested they drive to see her college campus. "You and your mom did the tours, but I never did. I'd like to see where my hard-earned dollars are going."

"Shouldn't we invite Mom?"

"Your mother knows all about it. We have her blessing.

Pull over here and input the address. Do you have it on your phone?"

"Yup."

Bill leaned his seat back several inches and told Chloe to wake him when they got close. He slouched down and closed his eyes. "I'm awfully tired from the week. Thanks for driving today. I'll just take a bit of a nap here. Remember, be sure to wake me!"

For the first couple of minutes, Chloe kept looking over at her dad, but at every glance, his eyes were closed. His trust dumbfounded her. Once her mind settled down, she realized the responsibility that was hers. She straightened up and gave her full attention to driving, her hands gripped on the steering wheel. Before long, she heard her dad snoring.

For a minute, she wasn't sure what to do. He was tired, but she thought he ought to pay attention. She let him sleep for ten minutes, then nudged him with her elbow.

"Are we there?"

"Dad, I think you're supposed to be alert when I'm driving, aren't you?"

"Are you doing okay? Any problems?"

"No. It's all good."

"You're eighteen, Chloe. You're an excellent driver. I have full confidence in you. Nothing will teach a young person to drive better than to be given serious responsibility. Your mom says you're a fine driver, and you aced all your tests."

"All Mom does is scream at me."

"Go easy on your mom. After what happened with your friend, she deserves a pass. When you're a mother, you'll understand. Speaking of that, how are things going with that Harold boy?"

"You mean Howard?"

"That's quite a name for a boy. Is he sixty?"

"Howard's long over, Dad. They named him for his grandpa. You gotta keep up. This week I'm single and content. Check in next week." She looked at him and smiled.

"Get your eyes back on the road, driver! You only have until Monday."

"What do you mean?"

"Your mother reserved an appointment for your test on Monday. You have to be ready by then."

Her dad slouched back down and closed his eyes. He told Chloe to wake him when they got close to Milwaukee.

The Pink House

L aura's three-bedroom home stood out on the block because of its color. Typical for the neighborhood, the two-story house had a two-car garage with doors opening to the front. It was the only pink house in the area.

Laura always spoke about her home using words such as comfortable and lived in. Mallory, her neighbor across the street, thought of words such as filth and dirt whenever she entered Laura's house. Last week when Laura had beckoned to her from the driveway to come and try the jam she'd bought at the farmer's market, Mallory found walking from the front door to the kitchen to be a challenging maze. She stepped over a blanket and around toys. It was almost impossible to take a step without crunching Cheerios, crackers, or whatever remnants of food lay on the unswept floor.

To be fair, Laura had three children, ages six, four, and two, but Mallory's mother had once raised three children of similar ages, and her mother kept an immaculate house.

Laura asked Mallory into the kitchen and invited her to sit down. Mallory looked at the five chairs around the kitchen table, trying to find the one that might be easiest to clean off.

"Where would you like me to sit?" she asked.

Laura grabbed a stack of books and some clothing from one chair and dropped them on the floor a few feet away. After Mallory brushed crumbs from the seat and sat down, Laura plopped jam on the table with a knife sticking out of the jar. She served Mallory a slice of toast on a paper plate. It relieved her to see the disposable plate, but noticing stacks of dirty dishes around the kitchen sink area, she realized paper was probably the only option.

When her mother taught her as a child to always eat what a host places before you, she doubted anyone had served her mother from a kitchen as dirty as this one. Laura sat down across from Mallory after cleaning off a second chair using a similar method as before.

After serving the toast and jam, Laura said, "I have a question for you. Things are getting a little crazy around here. I'm taking a trip to California to attend a conference. I need to get away for a bit. I've sort of been thinking that we're all in this life together. Wouldn't you agree it's important as neighbors to lean on each other for help?"

Mallory nodded, not knowing what else to say.

"I could use your help with the kids in order to take this trip. My friend and I talked, and we think that as a woman without children, you have a responsibility to help those who do."

This was a new low. Mallory thought of the time she received a call from someone at her church who suggested she head up the Mother's Day banquet since she didn't have children.

Mallory wasn't without children by choice. Two adoptions had fallen through after she and her husband experienced three miscarriages.

After the third, Mallory and her husband moved forward with their lives. If they gave birth to a baby, that would be great, but if not, they would be okay. After all, their marriage was a happy one.

Laura said, "I've seen your house, and I know you have extra bedrooms. I'm headed to a conference in California. We leave in ten days, and I'm wondering if you could take my kids while I'm gone. Or you could come over here and stay with them. That would work even better."

"What about Scott?" I asked.

"Oh, he's coming too. Didn't I mention it was a couples' getaway?"

"I have my job."

"Don't you have Fridays off? I thought last time we spoke you said you work long shifts Monday through Thursdays so you can have Fridays off. My mother could meet you here on Thursday night and drop the kids off, and I'll be back for them either Sunday night or Monday morning."

"I head to work at seven on Monday mornings. I don't think that'll work out."

"Okay, Sunday night then, by midnight. The flight gets in at ten thirty at night on Sunday. I am counting on this trip for a break, and I don't have anyone else to ask. At her age, my mom doesn't think she can handle more than a day or two. Don't you think, since you don't have kids, you could help me out just for a few days?"

Mallory wanted to say that her mother never needed time away from her children. She wanted to say her mother would never have allowed her home to fall into such a state, but she heard herself saying yes. But the kids would need to stay at her house. She insisted.

Mallory knew she could never sleep in a house with who-knows-what crawling over it. She decided she would enlist her husband's help, and while the kids were watching television or sleeping, she would head over and introduce Laura's home to a vacuum cleaner, a mop, and a bucket. It would be easy to come up with an excuse to get the keys from Laura.

When the weekend was over, Mallory planned to read some books on how to say no in difficult situations. And maybe it was time to move. Her husband had been after her to look at homes with him for over a year. Maybe it was time to stop resisting. She picked up her phone to give him all the news.

A Song in the Middle

Her husband's timing could not have been worse. Zach moved out of their house the Saturday before Thanksgiving. She wondered if he'd be bold enough to take his new girlfriend to his parents' home for the holiday. Sadie would spend the day by herself.

On her income alone, Sadie wasn't sure she'd be able to afford to stay in their new home. She worried about that a lot. They bought the house last year when they moved to Arizona to be close to his family's side. She'd moved eighteen hundred miles from her friends and family because a company offered Zach a job in Phoenix. He wanted to live near his family. For his sake, Sadie left a job she loved. Less than a year after their move, Zach told her he was leaving her for an old girlfriend.

For more than two years, Sadie and Zach had saved and planned for a vacation to Fiji. A friend who works with her husband phoned her and told her that Zach and his girlfriend, Angela, were taking the trip she'd dreamed of. Right after Christmas. How had she married that sort of man? What kind of person does that to his wife?

Now she would spend Thanksgiving alone. She could handle that, but she couldn't bear the thought of being alone on Christmas Day. But that's how it would be. She couldn't get more than a day or two off work at Christmas. She was new at her job and hadn't built up vacation days yet.

Sadie called her mom and broke the news about Christmas. Her parents couldn't hop on a plane to come to see her. They were hosting a houseful that day. Her grandparents, her two older sisters and their families, and an aunt would gather without her.

Sadie survived Thanksgiving, thanks to a wonderful book and her favorite TV channel. Two days before Christmas, she walked down to her mailbox. On her way back up the drive, her neighbor waved and approached her.

"I'm Toni from across the way. I'm delighted we're finally meeting. Sorry I haven't been over sooner. Some health issues have distracted me." Toni reached out, and the two shook hands. "I know you may have plans, but just in case, I'd love to invite you and your family over for a meal around two o'clock on Christmas Day. My husband passed away a few years ago, and I miss having someone to cook for. A few of the neighbors will join me. People seem to like to eat what I make, and I love to cook. Please join us if you'd like to come."

Sadie explained that her husband had recently moved out. Because of the woman's kindness and warmth, Sadie gave in and accepted her invitation. She wasn't excited about spending Christmas with strangers, but she dreaded being alone on Christmas. Sadie had never been good in large groups, but she decided at that moment that almost anything would beat being alone for the day.

On Christmas Day, because Toni was such a terrific host, Sadie's feelings of awkwardness disappeared within the first minutes. Everyone was kind to her. She enjoyed a beautiful afternoon. As she left that night to head back to her place, she turned to Toni, hugged her, and thanked her.

"Being included today meant a lot to me. My husband left me last month, and my family lives over twenty-four hours away by car. I couldn't get the time off from my new job to go to them, anyway. The food today was wonderful. And I love my gift. Thank you for having me."

Back home, Sadie set her timer for an hour. For too long, she'd taken a break from picking up her home. She caught herself humming as she worked on tidying up her kitchen. She used to sing all the time, but as she heard herself hum, she realized it had been a while. Too long. She took a big breath and sang the first song that came to mind. It wasn't a Christmas song, but as she listened to the lyrics, she smiled.

Shopping for Next Year

We pull into the cemetery, pretending we won't need it soon but fearing we will. From the back seat, my sister, who is also my best friend, asks my husband what color headstone he likes best. It's her way of trying to find out what color I like best since the doctors have warned me that I may be in the market for one sooner than I'd hoped.

I point out two black ones and mention how ugly they are. It's my way of making sure the headstone will not be black. I say I think any other color will be fine. But I don't care for the salmon ones either, so I say, "Salmon has never been a wonderful color on me." I look around for the shade of pink stone I'm hoping for, but I don't see one in this small cemetery.

My husband says he thinks they're all fine. That's his way of saying it's my choice. I know he'd be fine with cremation because it's easier, but I won't have it. I've learned he believes in honoring deathbed wishes, so I'm sure I'll get my way.

The prettiest one I've ever seen is Aunt Patsy and Uncle Jack's pink stone they bought twenty years ago. I admired it when we were in their cemetery for another burial. Their stone is in place, ready to go when they are, but they show no signs of departing. They're thirty years ahead of me, but if my doctor gets his way, I'll need mine first.

I think how unfair it is that death does not strike in chronological order. I can't think of a dignified way of verbalizing the thought, so I wonder aloud if Jack and Patsy would loan me theirs for a time. It's a beauty.

Being Understood

Savannah couldn't explain her mood. Saturday was usually her favorite day of the week. She and Seth ran errands, cooked lunch, and took a long walk together. The weather was perfect.

"It's been a good day. I can't figure out why I feel so sad," she said as they emptied the dishwasher together. "It's like life is pressing in on me."

"I think I know."

"What?"

"This afternoon while I was replacing the light fixture, you watched part of that show. The one where the mothers give birth. Could that be it?"

The couple had been through years of trying and

waiting. There was the first failed adoption. When the second birth mother changed her mind, they'd chosen to move forward with life and accept the current size of their family. They didn't talk about their childlessness much anymore.

Savannah knew Seth was right as soon as he spoke. "Maybe you're right."

Less than an hour later, she caught herself smiling. The mood had disappeared. She didn't have the children she'd longed for, but being married to a man who understood her was a tremendous comfort.

The Peephole

Krista could hold still as long as needed. No problem. With her eye pressed to the peephole of her door, she had the perfect view to keep watch on the apartment across the hall. Her future was at stake, after all.

She held her eye to the hole without moving, determined to avoid the chance the peephole would appear to change from dark to light and thus reveal her position. She didn't want her new neighbor to think she was nosy, even though she had an extra-strong tendency toward curiosity.

Which of the six people she'd seen going in and out of the apartment would be new neighbors, and which were just family or friends helping for the day? Would it be a single person or a couple? Old or young? She wanted to know as much as she could as soon as possible.

Krista had counted four males and two females. The two women looked about her age or a little older, and she dared to hope one of them would move in. Working from home limited her opportunities to make friends, and she'd love a close girlfriend.

She witnessed the hauling in of mismatched second-hand furniture, beanbag chairs, huge stereo towers, and a twin mattress with no frame. Her strong hunch was that one of the younger men would be her new neighbor. She let go of her hope to make a new friend close to her own age.

Her longtime friend Mr. Jacobsen had moved the week prior to a city three states away in order to live closer to his daughter and grandchildren. How she would miss Mr. Jacobsen! Such a kind, tender soul. He'd been the perfect neighbor, often telling her how much he enjoyed her piano playing and that of her many students but scarcely making a peep himself.

She would especially miss their Sunday evening get-togethers. Mr. Jacobsen had been coming over for ice cream at eight o'clock on Sunday evenings ever since Krista's younger sister moved out twelve years ago to get married. Krista couldn't remember how the tradition started, but he provided the homemade ice cream, and she hosted, setting her table with an ironed tablecloth and some of her mother's special serving dishes.

Quite the hostess in her day, her mother left behind multiple sets of china and elegant serving dishes for Krista and her sister to split between the two of them. Krista could host her Sunday guest many weeks in a row without ever duplicating tableware. She loved that Mr. Jacobsen made a fuss over her choice of linens and dishes each week. Her mother would have adored him.

The 104-piece Royal Doulton dish set Krista's family always used on holidays, the ones Krista loved most of all, went to Jenna after the two sisters flipped a coin. But Krista still possessed many beautiful dishes and was content with what she'd inherited, though she'd rather have her mother back on earth with her than possess all the tableware in England.

She stored her mother's dishes in her oversized second bedroom closet. Krista relished unpacking different ones every Sunday as she prepared for their ice cream socials and enjoyed regularly using her inheritance.

Over the years, the two had included other neighbors now and then on Sunday nights, but the building had a quick turnover. Now that Mr. Jacobsen had moved, she was the longest-lasting resident in the sixteen-unit structure.

The hallway appeared empty at the moment, so she pulled her attention from the peephole, stretched, and walked around a bit. She'd made several batches of cookies earlier when she heard a new resident would arrive, but she wanted to time her cookie delivery well for maximum information gathering. The more she could learn about her new neighbor, the better.

She wondered if her china platter held enough for four men and two women. They'd been hard at work and might be hungry. She carried the plate back to the kitchen and added another dozen. Her mother always advised it was far preferable to have too much than not enough when you're serving food.

Krista opened her door and cleared her throat just as she noticed the two women heading back into the apartment. They propped the door across the hall open, and Krista caught their attention without knocking. She introduced herself and soon learned she was speaking to the mother and aunt of the new tenant. They'd traveled three hours that morning to help Sean with his move. The older men were husbands of the women, and Sean's cousin had come along to help.

Sean would start a new job on Monday, his first since he'd graduated from college. Turns out he'd taken an unwanted gap year but found work after a lengthy hunt.

"That just goes to show you how critical persistence can be," Krista said. "I so admire people who persist when things get tough. Congratulations!" She held out her hand to the mother and smiled at her. "I'm sure you're very proud of your son."

Just then, one of the young men walked in carrying a large, odd-shaped box. He set it down, wiped his hands on his pants, and shook Krista's hand after his mother blocked his path, pointed toward Krista, and introduced the two of them.

Krista wished Sean well in his new home and said she hoped he liked ice cream.

"It's my favorite food. Ask anyone."

His mother nodded.

"And look what she's brought for us," said the aunt, holding up the platter she'd accepted from Krista.

"Mr. Jacobsen, the man who lived in your apartment, used to come over every Sunday night at eight o'clock for homemade ice cream." Krista didn't mention that he made the ice cream each week. She was pretty sure she could figure it out. How hard could it be? She invited Sean over for Sunday night and mentioned she'd be trying out a new flavor.

His mother and aunt commented how nice it was of Krista since Sean didn't know a soul in the city yet. Of course, they knew he'd meet people once he started his job, but it might take a while to make friends.

"Will tomorrow night work for you, Sean?"

He nodded.

"Just come across the hall and knock at eight o'clock.

I have to head out now and run some errands, but I look forward to getting to know you better over ice cream."

Krista went back to her apartment, and forgetting about watching at the peephole, she looked up the ingredients needed to make homemade ice cream. She decided on mint chocolate chip since it had been Mr. Jacobsen's specialty. He was only a phone call away if she needed his advice. It was time to hear how he was getting settled in at his new place, anyway.

Locking her door behind her, she headed out to shop for a new electric ice cream maker. Afterward, she'd go to the grocery store to purchase the ingredients for her new ice-cream-making adventure.

Mathematical Advantage

The gray, misty weather matched Dana's mood. She'd had almost fifty years to prepare for the inevitable, but here it was upon her so ridiculously soon. She didn't mind that she'd be turning a half-century old in less than a week. At least, that's what Dana kept telling herself.

What bothered her was no one had planned anything special for her milestone birthday. Turning fifty was a pretty big deal. If her parents were still alive, they'd have done something special. They had always come through.

Since her birthday fell on a Saturday, she wouldn't even get to see her work friends that day. Sometimes they brought donuts in for birthdays, and her co-worker Jessica might have made a sign. She just couldn't bear thinking of spending the day alone.

Maybe she'd go hang out with her brother and his family. She might even stay overnight. They were always crazy busy, but she knew they'd welcome her, and they would try to treat her special as they hurried around. That's all she needed. Just someone to care.

The phone rang, interrupting her thoughts. Her brother started singing the birthday song. When he finished, she said, "Thanks for thinking of me, brother, but you're four days early."

"I know. Sorry, but I'm on my way to Singapore for work. The time change and my work schedule might keep me from calling. I'm in the car right now on my way to the airport. I just wanted to wish you a happy forty-ninth birthday. Sorry I didn't buy you a gift. This call will have to do. Aren't you delighted to hear my charming voice?"

"Delighted, I'm sure," she said. She stood in her kitchen and curtsied to no one in particular. "But I'm afraid you're quite behind the times. I turn the big five-oh this year, baby brother!"

She and Jason had grown close, especially in the five years since their parents passed away. When her husband of twenty-eight years left her, Jason had been there for her. He and his family really stepped up.

"Sorry, Sis. I'm afraid you're going to wait another whole year to break that steel barrier."

His comment met with silence. After a moment, Jason continued, "What year were you born, Dana?"

She answered.

Jason broke another long silence. "Are you doing the math?"

"You know I stink at math!"

"It's going to be worth the effort. Do you know what year it is?"

"Yes. I may be old, but not that old."

"Well, please let the current senior accountant of his company, who was also once president of his high school math club, help you out. I'm delighted to present you with the gift of an entire year of life. You're not turning fifty this year. You're forty-eight right now, and in a few days, you'll be forty-nine. A mere forty-nine years old. That's all."

"No way!" she said in disbelief. He gave her some more time to let the truth soak in. "Without Mom and Nick around, I haven't kept track of my age as well. And the divorce shook me up pretty good, you know."

"Are we on the same page now?" he said.

She nodded.

"Are you nodding? You've always been a nodder."

"Yes! I think I'm going to cry. This may be the best gift ever. I think turning fifty was bothering me more than I would allow myself to admit."

"When fifty comes, I'm throwing a big dinner for you.

Whatever restaurant you choose. It's on Sharon and me. But for now, enjoy your forties for another entire year."

Dana sniffed and wiped her tears with her sleeve. Then she laughed. It felt good to laugh. "It may be a wonderful week after all."

She told Jason maybe she'd ask a friend to see a movie or something for her forty-ninth birthday since he'd be out of the country. "And tell Sharon she doesn't have to do a thing for my fiftieth. She's always so busy. I'll help you with all the details."

After their call, Dana dropped her head in her hands. After a few seconds, she stood up, put her hands on her waist, and danced a jig right there in her kitchen. Now she'd have an entire year to help Jason plan her party. Her brother was beyond generous, but he'd need plenty of guidance.

A Stepmother's Visit

❝Maybe another weekend would work better once the house has a floor again. Everything's a colossal mess. We're removing the tile. After we remove the old stuff, we'll start laying the new flooring. In the meantime, we're living in chaos."

Married for two months, the young couple decided to replace all the flooring in the old house they'd purchased. Mid-process, they doubted the wisdom of the endeavor, as any newlyweds might.

"I could come and help," the husband's stepmother said. "I'll cook some meals for you and freeze some too. I'll stock your freezer with a month's worth of meals."

"It's an eight-hour drive."

"I know. I have a week off work, and William will be in Toronto on business, so I may as well spend the time with you two.

The young couple couldn't afford a hotel for her but offered it anyway since she seemed so determined. "Nonsense! No need to waste your money. I'll stay with you. I'm sure I can find a corner to lay my head."

"We've moved the appliances out of the kitchen to remove the floor. The fridge is in the living room, and we've unplugged the rest of them."

"I could help with laundry."

"We've unplugged the washer and dryer. The house is a dusty mess. You can't imagine how stubborn the tile is when we try to remove it. Refuses to come off until we hammer it and pick up the pieces. Even a crowbar isn't much help. How about another weekend? Maybe in a month or two? You should visit us then, and we'll be able to enjoy our time with you."

"It sounds like what you two need is help. I'll be there Friday at three o'clock."

"We don't get home from work until six o'clock, and we only have the one bed."

"I can sleep on the couch."

"We have a bunch of things piled on it, and it's covered with tarp because of the dust and debris."

"Sounds like I'll beat you home, so leave the door unlocked. I can't wait to see your new place. I have the address. See you Friday."

Clearing the Dishes

Everyone who ever attended summer camp at Camp Grey knew of Deanna Dunn. The story about her losing the contents of her stomach when tasked with clearing her dishes after meals was legendary.

The misfortunate occurrence happened three times before they permanently excused her from clearing her dishes again. Camp janitor Mr. Gus demanded the policy.

Deanna's stomach didn't object to rinsing off dishes when she was at home. She didn't have a problem with washing dishes for her family either when another family member rinsed them first.

The sight of dirty dishes stacked in a large black tub

with the bits and pieces of strangers' food smeared every-
where was enough to activate her gag reflex. Even now,
when summer camp was a distant memory for her, she
had issues at the serve-yourself style restaurants where
you're expected to clear your own dishes.

In adulthood, whenever their family eats at such a
restaurant, her husband clears her dishes for her. As she
exits restaurants, if the busing station is near the door, she
averts her eyes as she passes.

On Friday, Deanna and two of her co-workers dined
at just that type of eating place. The two headed up a
project she was eager to be involved with, so she wanted
to impress them at the lunch. Deanna hoped to join their
team for the duration of the project.

Deanna was so used to her husband helping her out
by clearing her dishes, she didn't give the matter a thought
until it was time to go. She stood first. "I'm going to clear
my dishes. I'll be right back."

As she stood and picked up her plate and almost-
empty salad bowl, one of the other women said her ankle
was bothering her and asked Deanna to carry her dishes
for her. "I hope you don't mind," she said.

Deanna nodded. She didn't know what else she could
do. The woman piled her plate on top of Deanna's and
set her bowl on top of the bowl in Deanna's other hand.
It didn't seem the other woman liked her food. She'd left

half of it on the plate in the opposite of a tidy manner.

Deanna walked as fast as she could to the busing tub. They stationed it in the back near the kitchen door. As she approached, she turned her eyes upward. She planned to avoid seeing the bins until the last second. As she reached the station and glanced down, a black tub heaped to over-flowing with dishes met her gaze.

There was no way she'd fit more dishes in without some rearranging, and that would not happen. Deanna looked underneath. The diners also packed the lower cart shelf full of dishes. She held her breath, careful not to take in any of the strange smells. Just when she thought she wouldn't be able to control what seemed inevitable, a worker came up behind her.

"Here, let me take those from you." The worker spared Deanna the trouble of figuring out where to put the dishes just in time. As she turned away, a child ran in front of her, almost tripping her. This action had the blessed result of distracting her body from what it was considering.

The two ladies stood when Deanna returned to the table. She spoke to the one with the dishes left to clear. "The dirty dishes cart is jam-packed. You'll need to leave yours on the table."

Deanna said goodbye to the two women. They were in the middle of a conversation they'd started while she cleared dishes. The two lingered near the table. Deanna waved and turned toward the exit door.

As soon as she stepped outside, she breathed a huge sigh of relief. As long as she could keep the picture of the dirty dish bin from her mind, she would be okay.

The Day I Noticed Daniel

Daniel captured my interest the first day I met him. We were a group of six seated at a round table in the dorm cafeteria. Russ told a crude joke. He could be such a jerk. I noticed everyone laughed except Daniel.

Later, when Marcie walked past our table, Russ commented on her looks. He spoke loud enough for all to hear. Marcie is beautiful by anyone's standards. But Daniel didn't look as she walked by. Not even a glance. I decided that day he might be the guy for me.

Any guy with enough restraint to avoid gazing at Marcie when she walked by would be a man worthy of trust. I've heard you can tell a lot about a man if you watch his eyes.

Lillian

Lillian phoned Jeannette five days after the funeral to ask if her children had returned home. "You've been on my mind nonstop, but I didn't want to intrude when your kids were visiting. Have they all headed back home?"

"Charlie and his family left Tuesday. He had to get back to work. The girls and everyone else left this morning."

"I drove by earlier and didn't see any cars in the driveway. I'm coming over to help you with the beds and everything," said Lil.

"The girls helped with all that before they left, Lil. The house is clean, and it's so quiet I could hear a pin drop."

"Unless you're napping, I'm coming over so get the dominoes out. Or plan a job for me."

"I'll find the dominoes and heat water for tea. I'm absolutely exhausted, but my mind won't let me rest."

Jeannette won the first three domino games. She even caught herself smiling about the wins. It felt good to smile, but as soon as she became aware, pangs of guilt outdid her cheerfulness.

"I don't know how I'll live without Gary. I know it isn't helpful to think this way, but it seems as if he didn't deserve this. He was the cheerful one around here. Lord, he knew how to make me smile. What will I do without him?" She dabbed her eyes with a tissue.

"I'm sorry," Lil said. She shuffled the dominoes around on the table much longer than necessary. "You have three wonderful kids, Jeannette, and all those grand-kids. I'd miss you terribly and I hope you'll stay, but have you thought of moving to live with one of them?"

"It's too soon for a big decision, but I think I have my short-term plan. I'm digging my heels in here on Bel Air Drive for as long as I can afford the property taxes. The other day, Charlie invited me to come live with him and Jessica in Florida. Later the same day, Emily and Jacob said they'd have a room for me in Seattle, and Samantha says she and Josh would like me to come to Denver and live with them."

Lil raised her eyebrows. "This is a huge house for just

one person to take care of. What are you thinking you'll do?" After a long pause, Lil continued, "Who would you live with if you could choose?"

"The longer the kids talked about the possibilities, the more tense the atmosphere became. Before long, I changed the subject and told them I didn't want to talk about it anymore. How can I choose between my children?

I suppose when I think about it, it makes the most sense for me to go with Charlie. They have that enormous house, and their kids are almost grown. They even have an empty bedroom with its own bathroom on the main floor. That's where Gary and I stayed when we visited. They all sleep upstairs, so we'd have some privacy from each other. I think Charlie's place would work best, but I'm afraid I'd hurt the girls' feelings or offend them. I wouldn't do that for the world."

"Isn't it wonderful they've all offered to have you? Just think about that. How many parents can say that? I'm sure it's a tough decision, but you must be so proud of your kids. I guess they do always say to wait a full year before making critical decisions. Is that your plan?"

"First, I need to figure out money stuff. Then I'll decide. Right now, I hope to stay put for at least five years. The kids can come visit me here. I have room for everyone. I'm meeting with an accountant next Monday to get help.

"Why don't we try pinochle next? It's such a relief to have you here to get my mind off things," Jeannette said.

"I remember what it was like." Lil shuffled the cards as she talked. "It's been eleven years, but I remember well. The toughest days came once the funeral was over and the boys returned to their homes."

Before they finished their second hand, Jeannette put her cards face down, slumped over, and rested her head on her arms folded in front of her. She sighed a gigantic sigh. "I just remembered I have all those thank-you cards to do. The kids offered to help, but I kept putting them off. With everyone here, things were chaotic, and I need quiet when I write notes."

"Can I help? You write the notes and I'll address and stamp the envelopes?"

"I'm too tired to think about it right now. Maybe tomorrow," Jeannette answered. "Can you come by in the afternoon? I'm hoping to sleep in tomorrow—if I can even get to sleep at all."

"Sounds fine. You know, I packed a small bag. It's in the car. Why don't I run and get it, and I can stay in a guest room tonight? The house won't seem so empty then. In the morning, I'll run home and get my chores done, and then I can bring lunch over. Okay?"

Jeannette raised her head and nodded. Lil continued. "After lunch we'll write ten cards, then play a game, then write ten more. The games will keep our brains fresh.

I read an article about that yesterday. We could get the thank-you cards done in an afternoon. What do you think?"

Jeanette gave Lil a hug after they stood up. She'd been worried about how she would handle an empty house after the family left. Jeannette couldn't remember the last time she'd slept alone in the big house, but it was over a decade ago, back when Gary did some traveling for work.

"Let's see how well you sleep here tonight," said Jeannette. "If it goes okay, I may enlist your companionship for the next several nights, or just until I feel I'm able to handle things."

"Sounds fine," Lil said matter-of-factly. "I can sleep anywhere. You know me. I'll get my bag from the car, and then I'll fix some chamomile tea for us. How does that sound?"

Jeannette nodded her head. It was about all she had strength to do. She walked to her favorite living room chair, sat down, and put her feet up. She couldn't recall ever being served tea in her own home, but the teapot was on the stove, and Lil knew her way around a kitchen. Jeannette closed her eyes, and before the water came to a boil, she was asleep.

Used Cookie Sheets

The man living across the hall from Kendra opened his door as she arrived home from work. Mr. Vann, old enough to be her father, had lived in the condominium since she moved in five years earlier, and many years before that, she guessed.

"Remember a few weeks ago when I told you about Mother's passing? She loved to cook as you do, and she made the best meals. We never had money to eat out. Mother raised six of us kids. She cooked breakfast, lunch, and dinner in her little kitchen. The next day she started over again. Before Father passed away last year, they started eating out on Saturdays. Just the last year or two before Father passed. She loved that, I tell you!"

Kendra loved to cook, host dinner parties, and shop for kitchenware products. For several years, she worked weekends at an upscale culinary shop to avail herself of their employee discount. She'd stocked her kitchen with the finest cookware, cooking tools, cutlery, small electrics, china, glassware, and kitchen linens. Food was her hobby, and she knew how to prepare a fine meal.

Mr. Vann lived alone. From time to time, Kendra shared her food creations with him. Sometimes, she'd carry a dessert over. Kendra enjoyed feeding Mr. Vann— he always seemed so appreciative.

"Do you have time to stop over now? I brought some of Mother's kitchen things home with me, but I don't have room for most of them in my cabinets. Mother cooked all her life but never had fancy things. She deserved the best, but it wasn't to be. Not on this side of heaven. If there's something you could make use of, it will make me happy to know some of her belongings went to a nice place."

"Sure, now would be a good time. Thanks!"

Kendra walked into his home for the first time. Though clean, his bachelor status shone through. He'd covered his table with a layer of well-used aluminum pans, mismatched flatware, chipped casserole dishes, and cracked wooden spoons. Everything looked as though Mrs. Vann had used it for fifty years.

"If you see anything you want, you're welcome to it."

Kendra saw nothing that interested her, but she

didn't want to offend Mr. Vann or hurt his feelings, so she picked out two warped, browned baking trays. When it came time to make Christmas cookies, she could use more cookie sheets. "Here, I'll put these to use and think of your mother when I do. Thank you."

Kendra didn't have the heart to throw the pans in the garbage, which is where they looked like they belonged. She thought of the woman who baked for decades with these pans. Life wasn't fair. Why did a woman who labored to cook three meals a day and raise six children have to use such shabby pans? Why should Kendra own such fine things?

She opened the narrow, vertical cupboard that held her pizza pans, cutting boards, and cookie sheets back at her home. She cleaned the pans from Mr. Vann and stacked them upright next to her own upscale baking sheets. Every time she opened that cupboard to reach for a pan, she'd remember to be thankful.

An Unplanned Rest

J ackson switched lanes, cutting off other drivers, causing them to brake to avoid a crash. He relished pulling close to cars ahead of him and revving his engine. He taunted motorists until he got his way. Drivers pulled over to make space for him.

Jackson Dangerfield's wife, once a cheerful young woman, smiled little anymore. Not since her marriage. Her parents had pleaded with Molly, but she eloped with Jackson before they could stop the wedding.

This evening, however, Molly floated around her kitchen in a cheerful mood. The background music that often accompanied her dinner preparation was absent, though. She gave the meal her full attention. Everything needed to be perfect. Detailed planning began weeks ago. Tonight was the evening of execution.

To pacify Jackson, Molly usually fed the three girls an early dinner, then sent them to their rooms. The girls sometimes went to sleep early, but often they spent evenings together, tucked away in one of their bedrooms. The nine-year-old took charge, urging her sisters to speak in hushed tones so they wouldn't stir up their father's anger or draw his attention. But tonight, their bedrooms sat empty and quiet. Molly figured Jackson wouldn't even notice the girls' absence. She hoped she was right.

She checked on the slow-cooking beef stew. Molly would serve Jackson his favorite meal tonight as a tribute to her earlier dreams of happiness. He would enjoy the homemade rolls. Salad and pudding dishes waited in the refrigerator.

Molly took a deep breath as she heard Jackson's truck pull in the driveway. Here we go. Stay calm. She pulled the salads and desserts from the refrigerator. As he slammed his truck door, she spooned the warm stew into pasta bowls. Jackson expected to walk in the door and find dinner on the table each weeknight. Molly did her best to comply.

Jackson made his usual trip down the hall to the bathroom, and Molly pulled a bottle from her pocket. She squeezed one dropper full into his stew, then added an extra half a dropper for good measure since he was a large man.

Jackson didn't ask about her day or the children. He never did anymore. She kept quiet. They ate his favorite meal together in silence. Her eyes were on the clock tonight. After only eight minutes, he stood up and told Molly she'd better bring him a beer right away. He headed to the living room sofa and turned on a football game.

By the time Molly put the leftover stew in the refrigerator and loaded the dishwasher, Jackson was asleep. She checked his pulse at his wrist. You're being ridiculous. He's fine, she told herself. His snoring rumbled steady and loud, as usual. Molly covered him with a blanket. By the time he woke up, hundreds of miles would separate them.

She wondered for a moment what he would eat for future meals, but she shook her head. She couldn't think like that anymore.

Molly pulled the suitcases from the closet and loaded them into the trunk. She'd washed her car the day before. She inherited it from her parents when they passed away in an accident the previous year. Even though Jackson had taken much of her inheritance money, she had hidden some of it away. He bought himself a new truck and blew what he thought was the rest at the casino.

She'd determined not to take anything from the

house that didn't belong to her. Jackson could have the house. He could keep the furniture, the checkbook, and the credit cards.

She would take his girls, though. Yes, they were Jackson's girls, but she would take them. She would protect them at all costs.

When Molly picked up her girls, she hugged her dear friend and wiped tears from her eyes. "Thanks so much for all your help," she said.

This was goodbye forever, but only Molly knew it. She hadn't told the school. She hadn't told her friends. Revealing her plans might have put her or the girls in danger, so she chose safety above all. She would leave without telling a soul.

After merging onto the freeway, Molly found a talk radio station she liked and began the six-hour drive to the shelter in a neighboring state. Before long, her children slept, buckled in the back seat. She had telephoned the shelter in advance. They committed to housing all of them until she found a job and began earning wages.

Molly wondered if someone there could help with an identity change. She'd worry about that tomorrow.

Once Molly found a job, she would use the cash her mother had slipped her in secret several years ago after she'd noticed the bruises. Molly kept the bills hidden in her house all this time, stuffed in a duffle at the back of her closet. Though tempted, she never used even a dollar.

Her mother snuck cash to her, adding to the fund many times after that, but the two never discussed how Molly might spend the money. Her mother always said, "just in case," and they'd left it at that.

The duffle bag sat in the trunk now. The money would provide a minimum down payment on a peaceful little home for her and her girls. In several outings to the library, Molly had done some online house hunting. She couldn't risk Jackson checking her search history, so she never researched from home. At the library, she'd looked into shelters, schools, community safety records, and housing costs.

Molly's dream was to provide her girls a safe home with a backyard where they'd be free to run and play. She dreamed of the four of them sitting at the kitchen table, enjoying happy dinners together. Maybe they'd get a puppy. Jackson hated dogs, but that no longer mattered. She only wished her mother could see her now.

The Server

Having just recovered from influenza and a subsequent recurrence, I may have been on edge about germs that night, even more than usual. It was my first time at a restaurant in a month. I was near ecstatic about the experience. Eating excellent food and dining out at a new restaurant are two of my favorite things.

My good friend Klara had offered weeks earlier to take me out for my birthday once my cough settled down and my ribs recovered from the pummeling they'd received. As our husbands watched football together on a Monday evening, we did what we preferred.

When we arrived, she placed a small gift box on the

table and ordered a bottle of my favorite wine. I was thirsty, so I asked for water for the two of us.

The server brought us menus and a glass of water each, promising to bring our wine soon. He set the small tray of water glasses on an empty neighboring table, handed us our menus, and covered his mouth to cough, turning his head away from our direction. His cough sounded as bad as mine had the week before. He apologized, then picked up our water glasses, one in each hand. He placed them in front of us, removing his hands from the rims of the glasses as he set them down.

"Oh, dang. I'm so thirsty," I said after he walked away.

"What's wrong?"

"He covered his mouth as he coughed and then put his hand on the rim of my glass."

"I never notice such things," my friend said. "Here, have mine. We'll switch. I never get sick. You know that."

"He did the same with yours."

"Sorry. Let's ask him to get us fresh water," she said. "You're worried about getting sick again, and I can't blame you after the month you've had."

"It's too embarrassing. I'd hate to make him feel uncomfortable. Don't they train servers on basic hygiene anymore? I'll wait for the wine and hope that quenches my thirst."

"You'd be an awesome Hygiene 101 professor. I can picture it."

I smiled and excused myself from the table to use the restroom. It looked about as clean as a public restroom could look, and I had the room all to myself. I took some soap and scrubbed my hands for a good while. Using my elbow, I turned the faucet to cold.

Leaning over after rinsing my hands, I cupped them under the faucet and lapped up the cold water to quench my thirst. I helped myself to a paper towel and used it as a barrier between my hand and the door handle. When I returned, there were two empty wine glasses on our table.

My friend said, "May I pour for the two of us?"

I nodded. Thankfully, I'd been away from the table when the server brought our empty wine glasses. I decided denial was my best course of action. I pretended the server had held the glasses by the top of the stem as he placed them on the tablecloth. For good measure, he was abruptly and completely healed from whatever malady caused his earlier coughing spell.

Ray Loses His License

After his state refused to renew Ray's driver's license because he failed the vision test, his daughter Kimberly phoned and insisted he move in with her family. He could stay in their spare basement bedroom. It would make life easier on her. She'd no longer need to make the two-hour drive to his house each month to check on him. With the demands of her work schedule, the visits were getting impossible anyway, so she persisted with the debate.

"All of my friends are here, Kim. I've got my church, my doctors, and my bridge club."

"Dad, you know I prefer Kimberly. I've been Kimberly for ten years."

"Who do you think named you?"

"It's just getting hard for me to come. When the roads are icy, it's even more of a challenge. We have plenty of room for you. Why don't you try us? If you don't like it, you can move back. Maybe you can rent out the house for a year as we try living together? If you move here, when you need a ride, Mike or I can drive you. I think it will work. Mike is good with it too."

"My doctor says I'm doing fine. I've been on my own for five years now. I'm not sure it would work for us to all live together."

After more debate, Ray gave in. Maybe it would be nice not to live alone. Maybe things would work out. He knew he'd enjoy seeing the grandkids more.

Playing games became Ray's new favorite pastime once he lost the freedom his driver's license and car offered. His granddaughters, Hannah and Miranda, appreciated their new live-in partner for computer and board games at first, but they were both in middle school now, and once winter break ended and their extra-curricular schedule ramped up, they had little time for Grandpa. Ray taught them poker and pinochle to extend the game-playing, but in less than a month, it became a rare occurrence for him to persuade either of them to play any game. Even on the weekends.

Ray missed his friends from his old church. It had been tough to leave after forty-two years. He missed his neighbors, his back patio, and his grill. Ray especially missed his lawn work.

"I'd like to pull my weight and help around here, Kim," he said one spring morning after he'd been there a few months. "I still have some energy and life in me. Why don't you let me take over the yard work?"

"We hire that work out, Dad. Mike has never liked yardwork, so we've always paid someone. They do an outstanding job. You don't need to worry about it. Why don't you relax and enjoy yourself?"

"Okay, why don't I take over the garbage? I can empty all the wastebaskets in the house each day and haul it to the curb on Thursdays. I've noticed the trash bins go to the curb on Thursday mornings."

"Dad, the housekeeper does that."

"I guess that means no vacuuming for me either. Well, we have to come up with some job or jobs around here that I'll be responsible for. I feel like a worthless slug. I can't even drive the kids around for you."

"Dad, we didn't move you here so you could work for us. You should enjoy life."

"It's nice to be needed, Kim. I'd like to help. You and Mike work hard. I want to lighten the load if I can."

"It's Kimberly, Dad," she said. "We'll give it some thought and talk about it another time."

Ray read the senior center news each week in the local paper. He noticed they held video bowling tournaments, euchre Tuesdays, sheepshead Thursdays, and Friday chess. Ray knew he'd enjoy any of those, but he had trouble getting a ride to the senior center since it was on the other side of town. The center didn't open until nine o'clock in the morning, well after Kimberly and her husband headed to work. The center closed for the day at six o'clock, and since they didn't arrive home from work until seven or seven thirty each night, Ray couldn't go in the afternoons either.

Once a week on Thursdays, if it wasn't snowing or raining, he would splurge and take a taxi. The taxi dropped him off half a block from the center so he could walk and enter without being seen getting out of a cab. He could afford it, but he wasn't sure he should spend his daughter's inheritance on frivolities. And besides, taking a taxi was hard on his pride. He'd driven himself and his family around for over fifty years.

After he lost his touch at coercing the girls to play games, television became his new favorite pastime. When the girls came home from school in the afternoon, Ray let them control the programming. Because of hearing loss, Ray needed to turn up the volume.

"Grandpa, can you turn the volume down on the TV? I'm trying to get my schoolwork done before Mom gets home. It's so loud I can't hear myself think!"

"Why don't you go do your homework in your

bedroom, then come out and watch with me when you're done?"

Miranda groaned. "It doesn't work for me to do it in my room. I need the TV noise in the background. It's just too loud." Miranda covered her ears in dramatic fashion.

Ray turned the TV down, and after a few minutes he stood and ambled to his room.

The next day, Ray discovered how to enable closed captioning with the remote. He was excited. But when the girls got home, Hannah couldn't bear the captions. "Grandpa, the words cover the faces. I can't stand captions. Can we please take them off?"

"When the beginning credits finish rolling, the captions won't cover anything. They'll just roll at the bottom. I can't hear everything without the words," Ray said.

"They're just so annoying."

Ray discovered audiobooks after that. He found if he stayed downstairs in his bedroom and used headphones, he could download books and listen to them without bothering the rest of the family. It seemed to him the family was happiest when he was in his room, anyway.

One Saturday, as Ray emptied the wastebaskets around the house, he overheard his daughter on the phone with a friend. "I'm exhausted beyond belief. Between having two teenagers and being a caregiver to my dad, I have time for little else these days," she said. "He has an appointment at the end of the month. I have to use half a day of vacation just to drive him there. I love my dad, but caregiving is a strain."

The next Sunday, on the way out from church, Kimberly stopped and talked to one friend and then another while the rest of the family waited. People remarked over and over how wonderful it was of Kimberly to take her dad in and take care of him. Ray stood by. Some even turned to Ray to tell him how great living with the family must be. Ray smiled and nodded.

On Monday, Kimberly beat Mike home. Mike made his usual stop at the school on his way home to pick the girls up from lacrosse practice. Kimberly set the table and heated the food the housekeeper had left behind. She was used to her dad having the table set for them, so she called down to him, but there was no answer. She walked to the basement and noticed a note taped to his bedroom door.

Dear Kim, Mike, and girls,

Thank you for sharing your beautiful home with me. I love you all, but I miss my friends, my neighbors, my church, and my home. I've kept in touch with the agent who handled the rental agreement. The renters didn't stay the year, but I don't mind. I'm headed back to make things work without a car. Between friends, cabs, and the new private taxi service I just learned about, I should be able to make it work just fine. I know you're busy, so don't feel pressure to come down. Of course, you're welcome whenever any of you choose to visit. Be prepared to play a game or two.

Thanks for everything. You'll notice I took my things with me. I'll send a message once I have everything unpacked. I know Kim likes to worry, so check your phones. The agent looked the house over and says the place isn't in awful shape, so that's a relief. Any needed repairs I can't handle myself, I'll hire out. Love you!

Dad/Grandpa

Red Hair, Blue Hair

After reading for ten minutes, Jamie's husband turned out his light and rolled on his side to face her.

"Do you mind if I read for a few more minutes?" she asked.

"You showed amazing restraint at dinner tonight."

His shoulders shook, and they both laughed hushed belly laughs, struggling to keep the kids from hearing them.

"I think you're right," she said. And she winked at him.

"That's refreshing to hear. What do you mean?"

"The only way I could get through dinner was to keep staring at my plate the entire meal. I won't be able to look my son in the eyes again until he gets rid of that ridiculous blue hair. What was he thinking? Before your call, I had my lecture ready to go, but after some thought, I think you're right. The more attention we give, the longer we'll have to endure this. It's better if I keep quiet on the subject."

"Hair color is temporary."

"He's always had such gorgeous red hair. I love it. Why would he change his beautiful hair?"

"Your little boy is growing up. Might be time to relax the grip a bit, Mom. Remember all the bright sides. He gets good grades, he's respectful, and he has decent friends. A little hair color isn't worth losing sleep over."

"I'm going to miss seeing my son, but I just don't think I can look him in the face without cringing. I'm going to miss those beautiful blue eyes. Like Aegean Sea blue, but even better," Jamie said. "Remember the Aegean Sea?" She raised her eyebrows.

"I know. Come here." He opened his arms. She scooted to snuggle in next to him. "Remember the chicken pox, and the broken arm, and the time he needed fourteen stitches on his leg?"

She nodded.

"You'll get through this too." He kissed her on the forehead. "Now finish your reading. I need my beauty rest."

Jamie sat back up to read. Her bedside light never

kept her husband from sleeping. He'd be out in two minutes. Finishing her book might be the perfect distraction. She'd read it before but couldn't remember how the mystery ended. Too many thoughts whirled inside her head for sleep to come soon, but with both Agatha Christie and her husband on her side, she would survive this minor crisis.

The Retirement Cure

For the eighth time this month, Cara and her husband toured an open house. This time the home was for sale by owner. The owners greeted them at the door as they said goodbye to another family.

Cara's husband, Alan, headed outside to tour the acre-and-a-half lot. That left Cara alone inside with the woman. The owner shared that she and her husband had retired in the last couple of years and purchased an old home on Lake Michigan, up near Manitowoc, where many of her family and friends lived.

As Cara apologized from embarrassment for taking the stairs so slowly, she mentioned that her back problems likely resulted from stress, and she guessed they were only temporary.

The owner shared about her work as an occupational therapist. Though she'd suffered for years from bowel issues, headaches, and insomnia, her health problems disappeared once she retired. They hadn't returned.

"Retirement cured all of my health issues. Gardening gives me exercise and fresh air. We take time to cook healthy meals. I'm feeling great. The best I have in years. I can't recommend retirement enough."

When Cara arrived home, she took her ice pack from the freezer. While sitting in her chair to ice her back, she counted the years until her retirement. She'd never considered early retirement before, but her husband was three years older. Maybe she could stop when he did. He often mentioned the possibility. Cara decided to look into the details on Monday when she returned to work.

Birthday Lunch

"The special as usual, ladies?"

"We'll give the lasagna one more go, but Carol's on a diet again, so she wants the tuna plate," Barb said. She spoke for all four ladies, as she often did. "If your boss doesn't change the specials soon, we might have to switch our lunch date to Wednesday."

"Pot roast sounds good," Mary said. She pointed to her menu. "I see the Wednesday special is pot roast with a side salad and a roll. Is it tasty?" Their server nodded in the affirmative before hustling away.

"Mother used to make the best pot roast," Betty said.

Barb returned to the conversation they'd begun before ordering.

"For fifteen years I've never missed a single birth-day or Christmas, and do you know, never once have I received a thank-you note? Never once in fifteen years, if you can believe it! Not one time. I mean, not even a phone call. The kids are just like their mother. How much effort does it take to write, 'Dear Grandma, thank you for the birthday gift'? It doesn't even take five minutes."

"They have those thank-you stickers all preprinted out now," Carol said. "The kid just signs their name. I saw it on my morning news show. The parent fills out the envelope and everything. The child just signs, and it's done." She brushed her hands together twice as if dust-ing off crumbs.

"It's a different world these days," Betty said. "Mother would never even let us touch our gifts until after we mailed the thank-you notes."

"You're lucky, Mary. Your family is all so close," Barb said. "My grandkids are a thousand miles away, and I can't afford a ticket even if I weren't afraid to fly."

"I rarely get thank-you cards from them either, but they call and thank me, I guess," Mary said.

"I wonder if anyone sends a thank-you note any-more? Not anyone under thirty years old," Betty said. "Maybe no one under forty. Even a phone call would be nice. It doesn't have to be a card. Even an email would work. How much energy does an email take?"

No one answered Betty, so Barb continued.

"After a while you just think to heck with it." Her chin trembled, but she gained control and went on. "I'm done. From here on out, I'm done." She pounded her fist on the table, and some coffee in her full cup spilled down the sides. She hunted in vain for extra napkins on the table, then sacrificed the clean one on her lap to wipe up her spill and Mary's too. "I'm sorry about that, Mary," Barb said. She finished wiping up the mess before pulling a tissue from her pocket to wipe her nose.

"I'm just done. Where's the law that says a grandmother must buy gifts for grandchildren? I won't send gifts anymore, and then I'll see what they say. Let's just see what they say!"

"I wonder what would happen," Betty said.

"I'd like gifts for my birthday too, you know," Barb said. "The grandkids have never thought to send me a gift on my birthday. I've never gotten one card from them. They're just like their mother."

"I know Carol won't want any, but how about a slice of cake today for your birthday, Barb? My treat," Mary said. She picked up her purse and checked her wallet and said, "The cake is my treat today. I'm going to join you and have a piece too. How about you, Betty?

"I haven't had any birthday cake for years. Let's see if they have chocolate today," Betty said. "Thanks, Mary."

Barb waved the server over. After hearing the dessert choices, the three ordered chocolate cake to be served after their meal.

"I'll have a piece too," Carol said. "Mary, we'll split the cost of Barb's piece."

Later, after they'd enjoyed their cake and their fourth cup of coffee, Barb flagged down the server and asked for their separate checks.

"No check today, ladies. We've already taken care of it."

"We can't let you do that," Barb said.

"It isn't me."

"Taken care of by whom?" Barb asked as they all turned their heads and looked around the room.

"It was a customer who said they wanted to pick up your tab to add some sunshine to your day. That's all they said. Tip's included and everything."

"I'll bet it was that man sitting at the next table. Did you notice him doing his crossword earlier?" Barb asked her friends.

As the ladies stood up and put on their coats, Barb said, "You know, no one has ever done that for me before." She said it loud enough for all in the small diner to hear. The other ladies nodded in agreement.

"Well, happy birthday to me! That's the best birthday gift I've gotten this year. That man made my day," she said as she looked around at customers' faces, checking their reaction to see if it might have been someone else rather than the man with the crossword.

Her free meal was the only gift Barb had received

that year, but she kept that secret to herself. Mary, Betty, and Carol each brought her a card, of course. That was their tradition.

As the four ladies left the restaurant, the server brought two checks to a young woman seated alone at a nearby table. The server smiled and said, "How did I do? I didn't even look your way once."

"Perfect," she said. "You're awesome. Thank you."

The same woman rang her out at the front counter, and the woman handed her a generous tip after paying. "I'll have to try that again. That was my first time to do that sort of thing. Thanks again for your help!"

When the young woman arrived home from the restaurant, she phoned her grandmother before doing anything else. She thanked her at length for all the birth-day gifts she'd received from her over the years. Next, she sent her mother a quick text asking for family birthdates.

Afterward, for the first time in her life, she gave some thought to what she might buy her grandmother for her upcoming birthday. She settled on flowers and used her phone to order a bouquet of roses to be delivered to her grandmother on her special day.

Acknowledgments

I would like to thank Michelle Rayburn for her editing, cover design, typesetting, explanations, and guidance.

My special thanks to Kathy Carlton Willis for her editing help and coaching.

I am deeply indebted to the members of the Friends of the Pen writing group: Robin Steinweg, Anita Klumpers, Joanie Shawhan, and Sue Smith. You are wonderful encouragers, editors, and friends.

In addition, my gratitude goes to the *Used Cookie Sheets* launch team: Barbara Loch, Barbie Jusevic, Beth Anderson, Betty Rhodes, Cindy Beard, Hally J. Wells, Jean Crate, Jenni Lee Brocious, Karen Rothermel, Lien Polizzi, Lin Larson, Lisa Smith, Sally Ferguson, Shelly Krause, Sue Libey, Sue McLaughlin, Tracie Henkel, and Virginia Graves.

Finally, thank you to my husband, Mark, for the many ways he has supported me.

Dear Reader,

Thank you for taking the time to read *Used Cookie Sheets*. I hope you enjoyed the stories.

I have a favor to ask. If you liked the book, I'd love it if you would post a review on Amazon or wherever you purchased it. Reviews are vital to writers.

One of my readers recently sent me a list of her favorite stories from the book. I'd love to hear which story or stories you liked best. Your response will undoubtedly have an impact on what I write in the future. Drop me a note at Lori@LoriLipsky.com.

If you'd like more short stories, you can join my mailing list on my website **www.LoriLipsky.com**. I'll send a bonus e-book to your inbox.

All the best,

Lori Lipsky